TIGER TERWILLIGER

by

James L. Summers

Tiny Carleton High has been at the bottom of the football league for 8 years, so when their coach became ill, it didn't seem a great blow to competitive sports. Lanetta "Tiger" Terwilliger, iron woman mentor who crams Shakespeare down unwilling throats, takes over as substitute coach. Her colleague, Mr. Busch, doesn't know anything about football, but has a vast knowledge of volcanoes, and research reveals that volcanoes affect weather. Weather affects football, and with "Tiger" drilling the unhappy boys, their strategy is kill or be killed. Loren and his buddies are secretly trained in odd tactics by Mr. Busch, so that with the help of the weather bureau, gridiron history is made. Hilarious football story.

✣

Classification and Dewey Decimal: Fiction (Fic)

About the Author:

JAMES L. SUMMERS can't recall exactly when his interest in writing first developed. He won one dollar for a poem he submitted in a contest when he was in high school. It wasn't until after marriage, a degree from UCLA and two children of his own that he earned his second payment for a literary achievement — this time for a love story. Mr. Summers taught in the California high schools for many years. This gave him a familiarity with public education and young people. He left teaching to devote all his time to writing because he decided that writing sympathetically about young people at a time when the press was giving them a bad pounding had become a great calling for him. Many of Mr. Summer's books have been Junior Literary Guild selections as well as winners of special awards.

TIGER TERWILLIGER

F

gum

By *JAMES L. SUMMERS*

TIGER TERWILLIGER

CADMUS BOOKS

1966 FIRST CADMUS EDITION
THIS SPECIAL EDITION IS PUBLISHED BY ARRANGEMENT WITH
THE PUBLISHERS OF THE REGULAR EDITION
THE WESTMINSTER PRESS
BY
E. M. HALE AND COMPANY
EAU CLAIRE, WISCONSIN

2183

LIBRARY OF CONGRESS CATALOG CARD No. 63-13355

PRINTED IN THE UNITED STATES OF AMERICA

FOR GEORGE

TIGER TERWILLIGER

CHAPTER 1 . . .

As USUAL with Loren Wallace, the day had been sufficiently long and brutal enough already without added torture. Practice was over, and he waited outside the gym for Teddy Jacoby and a few other guys. He could get dressed faster than almost anyone else on the team, and he reaped fine rewards by having to wait around for slower buddies. In every life no matter how puny, he guessed, a little rain must fall, as the crazy poets said.

He stared blankly out over the sad little Carleton High School field. The rack of antique wooden bleachers had the unmistakable air that everything around here was going back to the reddish clay-type soil, but fast. Beyond and westward were the Santa Lucia Mountains, heavily wooded and nearly black in the gathering shadows of a gone day. They fitted Loren's dark mood.

Also a coming November already had its fell grip of fall on Del Obispo County, and he shrugged deeper and closer into his lined car coat, but with scrupulous care. Being second-string fullback on a team that barely had a first string was an honor, all right, but nobody could help preventing a few muscles from complaining about the agony. Every squad, however small, needed a few human tackling dummies to stand up and be counted when the chips went down.

At that moment, a flicker of lightning sheeted a piece of sky far back over the coast range and showed the veined depths of sullen clouds. It caught Loren's interest only because Carleton never had electrical storms, and the lightning was probably a mirage.

It was like his lost love—a moment of phony fire, then there was nothing at all but regrets. And wasn't that always the way? Around Carleton, life was merely past promises and no fulfillments.

"Vada," he muttered, letting her sweet name touch him with bitter memory. Even that small instant of weakness gave him a regular stab. Vada Long was about as remote as tropical splendor is from sour green apples. Once he had even dreamed of asking her to the Football Frolic which always closed the season, this year after the Almond Grove game. But that was impossible.

Right now he wished he hadn't even thought about her, because if it hurt muscles to get scrunched inside a car coat, thinking inside an unpinned skull was even worse. After a guy had let his head get plunged to earth repeatedly by characters such as Lardboy Tuthouse, Teddy Jacoby, Hodges, Martinez, and Sorenson, to name but a few, any style of thought came hard to a sprung brain.

Still, a person had to admit that Vada was worth thinking about, whatever the cost. She was both beautiful and good, even though she did love a few others, maybe. Also this year she was in about three of Loren's classes, and it was thus impossible to escape her mad charm.

At Carleton, naturally, there was no way to schedule stuff so a guy could disappear and forget, mainly because any one junior was in class all day with practically every other junior—not to mention plenty of seniors who hadn't got the message the first time around. Merely conditions.

This place was one of those forlorn little high schools trying to hang on to its individuality and not conform to

10

the masses. With only eight teachers to go around, there had to be some duplication. Sure, in a modern knowledge mill such as Almond Grove, five miles to the south, or Paso Verde, five miles north, a student could lose himself in the mob and never see a certain girl at all. But in Carleton you saw everybody merely by going through the front doors. Also, they saw you, which was worse. Loren realized that he wasn't exactly a vision of masculine perfection. He stood about even with Teddy Jacoby that way, and having to look at Teddy all day was enough to make the meek go and kill themselves.

"Agh!" he muttered in drear contemplation. But immediately afterward, he chuckled, "Ha-ha," like that. He was thinking of a line from a poem that Miss Lanetta Terwilliger had read to juniors that morning during English. "Think no more, lad, laugh, be jolly!" the poet had said. Wise words; he was trying to take that advice.

"Do it again," a drawling voice directly behind him suggested in a creepy style.

Loren sighed and turned slowly. It was Jacoby, all right. Anyone could recognize him with both ears shut in a dark room.

"Do what?" he asked tiredly, because he really was tired.

"Say 'agh' and then go 'ha-ha.' Do it, Loren. Try again."

"Why?"

"No reason, except you've probably got dementia praecox or paranoid schizophrenia, is all," Teddy said in sad farewell to a gone buddy. "I've been predicting it would get you, Wallace."

Loren had to nod. Could be; could very easily be. Any son of Dr. William Wallace, administrative assistant at Almabuena state hospital down at Almond Grove knew the terms, modern and old-fashioned. Dementia praecox was a form of insanity developed in late adolescence and characterized by loss of interest in people and things. Also by incoherence of thought and action.

He used a symptom right there and lost interest in Teddy Jacoby, whose dad also worked at the hospital as a senior psychiatric technician. Teddy's theory was that everyone—especially at Carleton High—was about to let go and snap, which was likely true. According to him, a couple of fine young youths succumbed every day, and the teachers had obviously all flipped years ago. He claimed that Miss Terwilliger, for example, had a strange fixation on grammar, Shakespeare, and the use of hypnotic educator eyeballs. Mr. Busch, who taught science and math, was completely dreamy and liked to get up on roofs to read anemometers for fun. Mr. Hipper, the principal, showed true signs of catatonic trance by staring out of windows and saying, "Why didn't I take engineering?" whenever school problems came up. A little thing like more trouble with the football team could make him do it, Jacoby said.

Maybe so, but a guy couldn't say that Miss Terwilliger didn't have a good grip on reality; that iron teacher had a grip on everything around here until it wanted to holler for mercy.

Besides, Jacoby went too far and included the outside world. For instance, in television ads he said that the one where the man came home from work ready to murder his whole family and then took an aspirbuff and loved them right away was a clue. It didn't show too much mental security, he claimed, and no use to tell him it was merely the business way in modern times.

Loren didn't argue; instead he changed the subject. "Where are the other guys?" he wanted to know.

"Lardboy just got out of the shower," in a morose tone. "Hodges is still on shoes. Somebody tied a couple of knots in his laces, or else he did it himself. Ever notice that Hodges is funny about shoes?"

"No," replied Loren, meaning not usually, although he did recall that Hodges always took a long time getting his laced. Also he carried a shoehorn with him wherever he went, but no comb. He would borrow somebody else's whenever he thought his half inch of bristly hair needed plowing in the mode. "Thanks," he'd say. "Whenever you happen to need a shoehorn, let me know."

By this time, Teddy was standing beside Loren, staring in the same direction. He was tall and lank in the shank, with a kind of Oklahoma accent in the way he was built. He looked as if he'd been put together by Cherokee Indians as a tepee.

"Good game last week, huh, Wallace?" Jacoby observed, viewing the field of glory. "The coach really had us fired up, I guess, or otherwise the score would have been different. Martinez and Sorenson were great. Even you did all right."

Loren warmed a little, recalling the fabulous scene. When Oak Hills High down near Valley City scored 31 against Carleton's 0, it was almost a miracle, and in their sports story even the Almond Grove *Informer* had been surprised. Usually Carleton didn't lose its games by merely a few touchdowns. They lost big.

Coach A. P. Blount had been genuinely pleased. "They had to use their second string most of the time," he'd said in his tough old voice. "Men, if you keep playing this heads-up football, next thing you know we'll be out of the cellar for the first time in six years. Or is it eight? Tuthouse, what does it say on the board?"

"It's eight years, Coach," Lardboy had bleated from the office.

"How time flies!" Blount had said. "Soon it'll be a full decade."

The coach was gray and fairly feeble now. He kept forgetting, but in earlier times, people said, he would have known exactly how long Carleton had been down there in last place. Yet Loren sometimes wondered whether he was actually forgetful or only amused in a wry style by life.

He taught U.S. history and government in his spare time, and even the government seemed to make him chuckle inwardly. A serious matter like the Battle of Bunker Hill could entertain him. "Some of the boys built a wall across the beach, you see," he'd explain in his concrete-mixer voice while drawing a diagram. "They sat there behind it, picking off the fancy British soldiers like ground squirrels. Of course, they lost the battle later on in the day." Blount seemed to admire a cheerful loser.

On the other hand, his son, Tom Blount, was coach down at Valley City at the south end of the county. This year, his third, he'd done all right, even getting a tie score with Almond Grove, which gave him an outside chance to win the league title for a change. But it was a long way outside at that, with only two games left for Almond Grove—Paso Verde and Carleton, both cinches.

Of course, Coach Blount's wild optimism about getting out of the cellar was another example of bad memory. This year the Carleton school board, with Hodges' dad as president, had almost settled the problem. The question of playing eleven-man football had come up for a vote again at Mr. Hipper's insistence and had barely won. Three board members of the seven favored joining the six-man league, with four against. A shift of one vote would make the difference.

Even that wasn't important when compared with the issue of consolidation with Almond Grove and a special school bond election coming up in a few weeks. Citizens, it was said, didn't want to send their kids away to school, but they hated to pay bonds almost as much. It was a true dilemma.

The truth was that Carleton High had to go the same

14

way as the American bison—toward extinction. It was only a matter of time, everyone had to agree.

Yet in olden days, this town and Almond Grove had been about the same size and bitter traditional rivals on equal terms. Then population growth had favored the southern town. The new freeway had bypassed Carleton and left it as isolated as a mining camp, with plenty of gabled and scalloped houses on tree-lined streets that looked like the dignified past preserved in a bottleneck. A visitor almost expected to see horses on some of the dirt streets, mainly because plenty of fairly good horses really lived there. A lot of people lived on small ranches along the Salinas River, and Lardboy Tuthouse, for example, was the son of Amos Tuthouse, who had once been world champion calf roper and still clung to the highborn equine memory. Furthermore, Almond Grove had been chosen as the site of the big state hospital, and that had turned the tide completely. Business moved south while Carleton stood still and tried not to slip back.

As for Loren Wallace, he lived there because his father liked it and had built a house on a few acres; otherwise there wouldn't have been any reason. Forward-looking taxpayers, who could tell a losing fight when they saw one surrounded by dollar signs, argued that instead of trying to build a new high school before the old one fell down, Carleton youth should go to Almond Grove. The school buses, they said, met and overlapped just a couple of miles out of town, and savings on gas, oil, and seat upholstery alone would be tremendous. Finally even some old-timers admitted that it was probably as inevitable as sidewalks, and progress had ruined a great place with a glorious past.

Loren came back to the present, mainly because Jacoby poked him in the ribs. "Seen Vada Long lately?" he wanted to know.

"Why?"

15

"You keep asking that," Teddy said plaintively. "Why, why, why. Because if you haven't seen her already, you're going to in about a second. She's coming down the walk toward us right now with Old Lady Terwilliger. So don't look around, Wallace."

Loren groaned. If there was anything worse than seeing that girl again, it would be to see her at the same time as Miss Terwilliger. The fine old mentor alone was almost too much for common eyes. He kept his back turned, but braced himself for the shock anyhow. They had to come this way to get to the parking lot, but maybe they wouldn't see him.

No luck. He heard the soft clop-clop of woman shoes, and the harsh cleek-cleek of teacher feet approach close and stop.

"Hi, Teddy," said a bright, cool girl voice. In a tone Loren knew was contempt for certain special men, she added, "Hi, Loren."

There was nothing else to do; he turned and faced them. "Uh—" he managed, "hello, Miss Terwilliger, and—"

He gulped, and even Jacoby took a little while to gain his customary poise. Lanetta Terwilliger had charged down upon them, and facing up to her on a guy's own time wasn't easy.

Her brute size was fairly normal for tall, thin teachers, although she'd developed a great set of neck tendons, probably by weight-lifting in the book room. What was awesome about her seemed to be a kind of fierce, intellectual karate that could kill a guy in one chop, although nobody had ever seen it actually happen. The sensation a person got from her was pure creature terror; she knew how to tame the animals anytime she wanted to make a few insane elephants and starved tigers sit on those little barrels and wag their tails. English from Miss Terwilliger wasn't a class; it was a crisis in a youth's short life. He got the distinct impression that everything else in school

16

from there on out was all going to be downhill.

"Good afternoon, Loren," she sang out in her rich basso-soprano. "How is football practice going? Ready for the Paso Verde game?"

"Fi—" Loren began, but checked himself. He knew by home experience that truth was the easier way. If a son tried to tell falsehoods, holler around, or be sullen, Dr. Wallace was likely to invite him to play a few sets of tennis to release hostilities and dispel resentments. Tennis with Loren's dad was like facing Chinese machine guns for fun and profit. "Lous—" he went on.

Teddy Jacoby leaped into the breach. "Just grand," he yelped in a style he used on teachers and people, letting his voice crack in true Oklahoma boyishness. "Team looks great. Wonderful scrimmage tonight with splendid blocking."

"Marvelous!" cried Old Lady Terwilliger. "I was telling Coach Blount today at noon that I hoped he'd drill the squad more on defense. We need to plug up some of the holes in our backfield."

Teddy Jacoby looked fairly sheepish, because everyone knew he was one of the biggest holes. Three Oak Hills touchdowns had gone through the right halfback slot which was his regular position.

"We certainly do, Miss Terwilliger, and—" The guy got a strange look. "And I'll bet we'd have the strongest defense in the league if you were coaching the team."

"If I were coaching the—Why, Teddy! What an idea!" She sounded pleased, as if the thought appealed to her. "But I'm not, of course. I'm only an English teacher, you know. By the way, boys, we start reading *Hamlet* tomorrow. Don't forget to take your textbooks home with you."

"Got mine right in my locker," Jacoby answered in a throaty voice, like a guy who could hardly wait to get his teeth into a book.

"Fine," Miss Terwilliger chortled back in the same style.

"Well, come along, Vada, dear. I'd better get you home before your parents decide we're keeping you at school far too long, even for the editor of the school newspaper."

They took off, punishing sidewalks, but Loren didn't move. The whole time he'd noticed that Vada Long watched him with her brown eyes half hidden by lashes. She'd had this enigmatic, faint smile inside her lips, unseen and sly. Mockery. Women had their own way of letting someone know how much they hated him.

When they were safely in the car, Jacoby made a small, twirling motion at his forehead. "Wallace," he said, "notice how she took the suggestion that she ought to be the coach? I tell you, stuff around her is balanced on the razor's edge. Miss Terwilliger may flip completely any minute now. It gets teachers; know that?"

"What gets them?" Usually it was the other way around.

"Stress," Jacoby said. "Strain. The turmoil of trying to cope with us merry youths from day to day and keep up with our vital, modern way of thinking."

"I guess," Loren told him absently. The door of the gym had sprung open, and he saw Lardboy, Hodges, and Joe come busting out. But before they could give customary greetings, the door opened again, and a head was stuck through.

"Tuthouse," said a hard voice. It was Blount, who started to cough heavily as if the name was in his throat edgeways.

"Yes, coach," Lardboy squeaked.

"Get back in here and pick up your towels," the coach said. He hauled out a handkerchief cut from square yardage, apparently, and blew his nose like a moose calling a true mate. "Who's your nursemaid when you're not here?"

"Sorry, Coach," said Lardboy. He scooted back inside without any more talk. Not picking up towels was a habit with him that was hard to break. Once or twice Blount had said publicly that he'd need to grow up, join the

18

Marines, and maybe even get married before he'd learn.

Tuthouse had gotten the name Lardboy back in grammar school when he'd been a sort of human storage vat for ever-normal grease surpluses. Now that he'd grown a foot or two he'd thinned out, but old-time fat traits still stuck.

Miss Terwilliger and Vada Long were just clearing out of the parking lot in the teacher's little foreign car, a good one that would do about a hundred miles an hour as easy as saying gotterrotterdam. Of course she lugged it along at about thirty.

"There she goes," Alice Hodges said scornfully. "Another of the great princesses of this here fair school."

Nobody around Carleton knew why he was called Alice, because his real name was Homer. Lardboy said it was because Hodges had an uncle who had once owned an Allis-Chalmers tractor, but that didn't seem too reasonable. Anyway, it had stuck, and by this time he was so used to it that his mother could hardly get his attention for trash-emptying chores and so on. Alice claimed it was because she called him by his real name, in a mother's style, and he always thought she meant somebody else.

In a way, it fit him. He looked quite a bit like an ape. His father owned the town's general merchandise store and was one of the proponents of consolidation, maybe because he thought his son wouldn't stand out quite so much in a larger situation.

Hodges had one other peculiarity: he was suspicious of all the women. He claimed they yakked all the time and did nothing but make trouble.

"Which princess?" Jacoby wanted to know.

"Vada Long," said Hodges. "Who else?"

"I didn't know. You could have meant Miss Terwilliger."

"Her?" said Alice in an ugly tone, which was his normal voice. A shiver of pure horror went all through him, and

19

on Hodges it was a sight to see. A person got the idea of what a night alone in the jungle could mean. "Cut that out, Jacoby. I meant Vada. And, say, guess where I seen that woman last Saturday?" He made mistakes in English purposely to confuse the authorities and throw off shackles. Having the president of the school board for a father didn't burden him too much.

"All right, where?" asked Joe Martinez, who was a big, easy-smiling guy with plenty of good nature. He had a lot of brothers and sisters, and his house was too small for bad temper. Mr. Martinez worked on the railroad and brought kids up to be courteous and get through high school.

"I seen her at the Melody Malt Bar down at Almond Grove," said Alice. "She was with some other woman, and Bobby Morgan. She was his date."

For one full second, nobody spoke. Morgan lived in Almond Grove and was the hottest back on their team. For a Carleton girl to go anywhere with him was like Martha Washington having lunch with Benedict Arnold.

"Don't believe you, Hodges," said Martinez, who was the one person in town who never called him Alice.

"It was Vada, all right. Think I'm blind or something?"

"Sure," said Joe amiably. "You're blind. Or maybe stupid."

Alice measured Joe with a hostile eye. "O.K.," he said harshly, "for you, I'm blind. But for everybody else, I seen Vada with Morgan. Not only do we consolidate while those guys take the women, but Morgan claims this year Almond Grove isn't going to beat us by their regular fifty to nothing. Bobby claims personal that this here year he plans to break a hundred."

It figured all right. Loren didn't say anything. Morgan was a rugged character and a natural athlete, so it was only logical that Vada would pick the best. He felt no particular emotion; he didn't have a chance against

20

local competition, let alone the whole outer world. If she were Morgan's girl, at least he wouldn't have to see her getting shoved by the neck around Carleton's halls in the familiar gesture of true love. She'd given her tender neck to Almond Grove.

Tuthouse came out of the gym.

"Hey," Lardboy said in a serious voice, "I think the coach is sick."

"Why? What did you do?" asked Jacoby.

"It isn't me," Tuthouse came back plaintively. "He just acts sick."

"How?"

"Dunno," Lardboy admitted, shrugging meaty shoulders. "He's different, somehow. Other times when he makes me pick up towels he sort of snarls in a friendly style. But tonight—"

"What's unusual tonight?" Alice asked. "I didn't notice nothing."

"He's weak, guys," Tuthouse said starkly. "He merely snuffled. Well, let's go. I'm hungry, and standing here starving to death isn't going to help the coach."

"No lie," Jacoby echoed. "What are we waiting for?"

Then Loren Wallace remembered why he'd been standing around all this time. His buddies wanted to ride home, and he had the car.

It was parked in the lot, a sedan too young to be classic and too old to customize. But it had one advantage—it ran.

They got over there and piled in, groaning from well-earned pain and trouble. Just before they took off, Loren noticed more lightning over the mountains. Yes, as Jacoby said, things were strange this year and likely to get worse as time went on.

But that was how life was for a junior at Carleton High. Rough. A youth had to haul back and accept and try to adjust to his own skin.

CHAPTER 2 . . .

LOREN KNEW that his dad's original idea in moving to Carleton was to live in the country and enjoy agriculture, and he had certainly got his wish. The house was on about ten acres of rolling land leading down to the Salinas riverbed and almost directly opposite the Long property, though shielded from it by cottonwood trees and dense brush.

There they had raised Walter, of course, and at one time Loren's kid brother, Fred, had owned a Shetland pony who didn't respond too well to good advice. Fred's pony liked to sneak up behind certain people and kick at them for fun, or he ran away with his rider and pretended he was going to jump the low fence. Special lessons from a horse trainer down in Almond Grove hadn't done much for Fred's pony, so he'd been returned to his former owner at an undisclosed price. Loren always suspected that his father had paid plenty to get the man to take back that little fiend in horse's shape.

Both he and Fred had also raised rabbits, pheasants, and a couple of drop-calves more or less to no avail—although rabbits did best. Dr. Wallace thought it was all good experience, not counting costs too high. But that was because he didn't have to go out every day and face sixty accusing Belgian hares who wanted to know how come the weather was so hot, and why they left Belgium in the first place.

Loren had learned that there were certain hazards to be worked out beforehand in agriculture. For instance, once a guy had raised his herd of nervous-nosed stock and seen it prosper, what happened next? Everybody in Carleton had his own private supply, so that even markets for giving away rabbits were unstable.

Worse than that, neither Loren nor Fred was ever going to forget Walter, who was one of the calves. Afternoons, when a person got home from school, Walter would be waiting at the gate. He'd follow a master right up to the back door, where he'd lie down and wait for a chance to sneak into the house. He probably wanted to hang around the big ranch fireplace with the rest of the family.

Amos, the other calf, who had been named in honor of Lardboy's dad, had followed more conventional bovine lines. He'd been sold early at a price nearly equaling what he'd cost in feed. But even Dr. Wallace had backed away when it came to selling Walter. "Fatten him up a little more, boys," he'd say, not quite meeting a son's questioning eyes. "He's not ready."

That was the real trouble with Walter: he never did get ready. Finally he became a family crisis, and once Loren had got up out of a sound sleep to hear his mother and dad using him as a conversation piece.

"Lillian," Dr. Wallace was saying, "what are we going to do about—about that animal?"

"Which animal?" Loren's mother had asked sweetly. "We have a lot of animals here, remember, dear? Rabbits, pheasants, and—"

"Walter!" said Loren's father in a kind of plaintive voice. "You know perfectly well which animal I mean."

"I suspected," she'd admitted gently. "But I didn't know. Those calves were your idea, Bill, and I advised you against buying them in the first place. But now—well, I'm sure—"

"You're sure of what?"

"That you'll know what to do with Walter. When the time comes, I mean."

"Oh, absolutely," Loren had heard his dad say in his confident style. "When the time comes."

Since Walter was already too big to be lying around a back doorstep lowing at eventide, Loren had gone back to bed thinking that his dad would take quick action. But he didn't, and pretty soon that calf was taking advantage and going up on the porch to lie down across the front door. It probably gave fellow hospital officials something to think over when they called evenings and found Walter blocking the way.

By that time, he wouldn't budge even if you talked to him nicely. He'd just stay there, sort of wagging his tail and mooing as if he'd gotten a personality transference and thought he was the family watch-cow. Sometimes when visiting psychiatrists wanted to get in while Walter was on guard, they had to sneak around to the back entrance when he wasn't looking. That always brought on plenty of joking explanations from Dr. Wallace.

Leaving the gate open while the family was on trips didn't help either. Walter was strictly a home bull and pretended he didn't know there was a way out, even after the gate got left open all the time. Finally, everyone was resigned to having him around as long as he lived, which could be twenty years or more.

Then one night last spring he must have had his feelings hurt, because the next morning he was gone. Nobody saw him straying around town loose, and he never came back. For a long time afterward, Loren would rouse at night when he heard strange noises, thinking that Walter had come home again like one of those faithful lost dogs of book and television. But he didn't.

24

Dr. Wallace and the family mother kept on talking about him even when he was but a memory. "You mean, Bill," Mrs. Wallace would say, "that you had nothing— absolutely nothing to do with—?"

"I told you before, Lillian," Loren's dad would say, "and I'll tell you again that I had nothing to do with Walter's departure. It just happened, I don't know why. Maybe he was an angry young bull who rebelled."

"Of course," she would soothe. "I believe you implicitly, dear, but there's no harm in asking. Walter has probably joined a herd of wild, free cattle up in the lonely, wind-swept hills, and—"

"Stop!" Dr. Wallace would say. "You're implying that—"

"But what did I imply?" she'd ask innocently. "I only said that I believed you. I have always believed you, Bill. I will go through eternity believ—"

"Now you cut that out, Lillian!" Loren's father would tell her, deep in his throat. "I had nothing to do with it."

The Wallace family had given up farming forever after Walter had proved himself a traitor and run away. Going through the open gate now, Loren thought it was probably a good thing. Some people were born farmers; others weren't.

He drove down the long driveway to the carport, parked, and stood on the rambling porch a second to look at the mountains again. As he suspected, there was no more lightning, and a fountain of stars had bloomed in the sky. In a way, he liked nature even though he was no good at agriculture.

Then he remembered that he was practically starved, so he hurried inside while he had the strength to open a door and barely made it across the living room to dinner. That turned out to be a fairly nourishing roast, apple pie, baked potatoes, and fresh vegetables picked from the supermarket.

When he'd got back a little energy, he happened to

25

notice Fred. The Carleton way was coming over the kid fast, although his brother was only a freshman.

The guy had said only one word. "Algebra!" Like that. But it was enough to show signs.

"How's that?" Dr. Wallace asked. "Did you say something, Fred?"

Loren glanced up. Sure enough, Carleton brain blankness had got another member of the family.

"No," Fred answered. "Not that I remember, Dad."

"I thought you said something like 'algebra.'"

"Not me. I—I wouldn't say a word like that. Not in the house, anyway."

Loren merely sighed; he knew—how he knew. Once his only brother had been a carefree, merry, husky little kid who was on top of grammar school heaps. Now the Carleton High School disease had got him when he was too young to fight back. Besides English, Miss Terwilliger taught one class of algebra, and with typical Wallace style, Fred had drawn the blackball. She had a way of teaching the subject where a guy learned what was called the "sentence of algebra" and he was lucky it didn't mean life.

Fortunately, his dad changed the subject. "How was practice tonight, Loren?" he asked.

"About usual," his son answered, glancing up. Once again it struck him that his father didn't look much like a psychologist or even a scientist—with this piercing, probing thirst for pure knowledge. He seemed more like a rancher with his tanned face, sun-crinkled eyes, and long, sinewy muscles which came from slamming tennis balls around almost every day to get rid of tensions. Real ranchers in Carleton appeared to be businessmen, and merchants dressed like rodeo artists, featuring boots and saddle pants. About the only people in town who acted like themselves were teen-agers, and they probably couldn't help it.

26

Dinner was over. It was Loren's week to stack the dishwasher. As usual, his mother stayed to help while Fred and his dad went into the living room to watch television. During football practice a player suffering from deep-bone fatigue was likely to put a spoon or a knife in wrong so that it slipped down and broke the impeller again.

"There," she finally said, moving a fork. "Now we can try it, and thank you, dear, for helping."

He made a small, weak gesture. A son liked to take some of the burden from old shoulders. "Don't mention it, Mom," he told her. "I do what I can."

She smiled in a strange way that he noticed. One gradually got used to having a mother in the house, so he didn't think about her as a daily routine. But every so often he wanted to know how age and strife were doing her.

In Mrs. Wallace's case, there wasn't much damaging erosion just yet—maybe because she'd had an easy life with all sorts of laborsaving machinery like this dishwasher. She'd gone gray in only a couple of spots and also still had good teeth. Compared with the general run of mothers hanging around family kitchens, she was holding her own and staying healthy and slim. He liked her, and sometimes her dark eyes twinkled as if she knew plenty of secrets—all of his, and a couple of her own.

"Are you tired, Loren?" she asked.

He was—about dead—but no use to let a weak woman realize it and start to pry into a person's intimate life. "No," he said, "at least not much."

"Then will you burn the trash, please?"

It was their stark system. They trapped an exhausted son into saying he wasn't tired and then they gave him plenty of labor to prove himself. But fighting it was useless. Like a true trash robot, he gathered their accumulated used wonder-packaging and stumbled into the night air toward the incinerator. One way he excelled around this house was in burning techniques. Fred had never got the full incinerator message and always left odds and ends around—butter papers, little cereal boxes, and empty matchbook covers. Because his dad was even worse, Loren suspected he'd inherited trash talent from the Lowell side of the family, which had been his mother's girlhood name.

He stuffed and lighted the pyre and stepped back feeling pure Lowell through and through. The flames stuck out hot tongues at him through holes in the metal while sparks got caught up on the fresh night wind. But they blew out safely before they hit the dry field grass.

They made him think of Vada Long. That was how their love had been—merely a spark from a lonely incinerator. It rose for an instant toward glory, only to fade away and never kindle a human heart. He sighed. It was a fairly poetic thought to come from just trash, but there was only so much inner poetry a guy could stand from himself.

Yet it was true in a way. Last year, when they were sophomores, they had loved for a brief season, or at least he had. Loren had gone into that class as merely a boy and been assigned a seat next to her. It was geometry. The whole year had been an unfolding of Vada's loveliness, inextricably mingled with the square of the hypotenuse and a couple of other things he remembered.

Man, yes! She had been everything a girl could be—and still was, for that matter, only more so. Kittens of light frolicked in her bronzy hair; the sweet curve of her cheek and throat, the tilt of her pert nose, and the depth of her golden-flecked eyes totaled the cube root of wonderful. She was pure girl, that woman, never to be duplicated in the whole world—at least not here in Carleton.

Also she had a special way of her own—a sort of catch in her voice and a common friendliness that was easy but not close. A couple of times she'd asked him to help her

28

with the crazy geometry lesson, and he'd done it, although she needed help about as much as Euclid, the Greek who invented the subject. Although she went out on dates with a lot of the fellows, Loren had got the fantastic idea that if he worked it right, waited and planned, she might some-day like him.

Vada had a strange effect on him. Whenever she was around a sort of awful paralysis gripped his presumed brain so tight he couldn't think or talk. She'd say ordinary Carleton chat-chat, such as: "The sophomore dance is coming in about a month, Loren. Are you thinking of going?" and it would take him so long to answer she'd lose interest.

He'd try to come back with some flashy remark brimful of the kind of teen-age wit other guys had. "No, I haven't been thinking about it," he'd begin, meaning, who had a skull working on future events at a time like this? "But—"

Then he'd freeze and have to sit there in silence for about ten minutes, trying to get back to normal and focus tiger attention on geometry. At that he barely got through the subject with a decent grade, and he hoped he never had to sit next to Vada Long again in his whole life. It hurt.

A few times she'd got mad at him for being so dumb, and twice she'd said: "Loren Wallace, you're a funny boy. I'll never understand you."

What woman like her would want to? At last the year had ended; being a sophomore was gone forever, and now as a junior he'd faced facts and stayed away from Vada as much as he could. He realized that she could never love the sort of youth travesty he happened to be.

Sure, he was passable in the common mob, Loren guessed. He was as tall as his dad, now that he'd got to be sixteen. But the resemblance stopped there. He had these queasy wrist and ankle bones hanging out, with everything else stretched so thin and weak that the whole improbable structure could give way like a house of shards.

He stirred a cloud of sparks and within them saw himself giving way—bending, breaking, and crumpling down in a heap of rumple clad merely in faded jeans, T-shirt, shoes, and a sad car coat. "Nice try!" people could tell his parents as they hauled the heap away. "He died from youth rot, probably."

Gamely, Loren put back his shoulders. He couldn't give up and die; too many coming events required his presence, and besides, dying of youth rot could worry his mother needlessly.

Instead, he took his father's advice and concentrated on the good. In hair he had the average nondescript bristles, and nature had blessed him with regulation ears hung fairly close to home. Also his one nose and solitary mouth were balanced off by merely two eyeballs. Luck had been with him there. Too, he had a healthy neck. A lot of people went through life with their necks giving them plenty of suffering. And his skull was adequate so that it didn't get singled out for unusual attention. One freshman kid this year could get a fairly tight fit in tin hats by wearing a funnel, and it didn't augur too well for good social experiences.

Yes, as his dad often said, a boy should be content with reality. Dr. Wallace had plenty of respect for the normal, well-adjusted average such as his son. He claimed that anyone working around Almabuena state hospital got to enjoying mere normalcy, and that gifted teachers should do it about six months out of the year.

The fire had burned down until it was safe to leave, but Loren lingered. If his dad could only know how far a son was from that goal—being merely average—he might worry a little bit too. But nobody was really concerned, and a person could only pursue his lonely way to the end.

30

A minute later he was back in the house. He washed away tell-toll smudges from trash work, said good night, and went to his room to hit the sack. Lately he hadn't been resting too well, and it was a rare night when he got in much more than eight hours of full sleep. He'd merely lie there and think. Insomnia!

Loren was wrong in believing that nobody was concerned about him. There were two individuals who worried profoundly, and he would have fainted with shock to know who they were.

One was pretty Vada Long. Ever since geometry, she had devoted much of her time to the riddle of Loren Wallace, but with almost no success. All she knew about him was that he was awkward, shy, intelligent, imaginative, talented, well-mannered, tongue-tied, and incredibly stupid. Oh, yes, and his middle initial stood for Lowell. She'd looked it up on school records.

Of these diverse and interesting qualities, this year he was radiating the last named even more than as a soph. Stupidity. If it kept increasing at the present accelerated rate, he would have it perfected and be the stupidest senior in school history.

This afternoon, for example, when she'd said, "Hi," to him in her most engaging manner, he had merely stood there with his adorable wrist and ankle bones hanging out. Naturally she would have enjoyed killing him, but what with being dead and all, he would be even more difficult to love—if that were possible. Instead she had continued to ignore his silly posturing just as she had been doing for most of the sophomore year and into the junior. It was all that any woman could do with Loren Wallace, as research among likely girls had shown, as long as he kept on being this way, his natural self. Yet in one sense it was comforting; Loren was likely to keep because he was girl-shy.

That fact was important. Long ago Vada had decided

he was the most desirable boy in Carleton, which at the moment meant the entire world.

One aspect about certain boys that she had been noticing since eighth grade was that plenty of them seemed to stay on at grammar school levels for the rest of their lives. Certainly they screamed around high school halls with deeper voices and described their glorious masculine selves with greater confidence, but their prospects for growing up seemed dim. She liked them in much the same way that some of her girl friends admired horses.

Loren Wallace was different. Vada doubted that he'd ever shoved a single girl around by the neck in his whole life to show his unquenchable love. He was quiet and a little dreamy, but there was a sense of the future about him that was mysterious and exciting. Right now, of course, he wasn't with it. No, indeed. In freshman social studies, for instance, she knew he'd stared out of the window for one entire spring with the intensity and dedication of a lapsed-time motion-picture camera. And, on a couple of occasions, she'd even fancied that he was going to flap his bony wings and take off through the screens.

Then last year she'd thought the time had come. The vacancy signs had come down from his dark, heavy-browed, menacing eyes. He'd taken to silent brooding until she half expected that he was sitting on eggs.

Once or twice, she'd practically asked him to invite her to school functions, so openly that she might just as well have hit him over the head. At that, it could have been the better way. A small, junior-sized hickory baseball bat might have got his attention. As it was, he only sat there sort of gasping for air like a bluegill with arms. Oh, she knew his trouble, all right. Loren was insecure.

He positively infuriated her. Truthfully, Vada wasn't so terribly secure herself, and a boy ought to take the initiative sometimes. Figuring out life against odds wasn't too easy for a girl either, whether she was reasonably pretty, popular, and successful in school or not.

Now at home across the riverbed, she paused briefly from study to wonder again why that impossible boy so disturbed her. She seemed to know a secret about him that constantly eluded any expression in words, so it probably wasn't worth saying anyway. Yet whenever she saw him a sense of fierce proprietorship came over her as if he were marked for her very own like a perfect house in early construction stages, not yet ready for occupancy.

Thinking that, she had to giggle a little. To see anything today in Loren Wallace took plenty of imagination about tomorrow.

Vada's father was a graduate architect who had gone into construction after learning the frail condition of architecture in Del Obispo County. Perhaps that had given her a sense of planning and explained why she bothered with Loren at all. In his troubled eyes, possibly she recognized instinctively something precious to women. But right now she certainly didn't know what that could be. He was impossible, stupid, boorish, and provoking. In other words, she liked him.

She sighed deeply and went back to her work with design and purpose. What Vada Long studied, she eventually mastered with one of the sharpest intellects in town. Only when she had finished the work did she go out into the living room. Her father was on the telephone, talking business, and Enid, her little sister, was watching television. Vada found her mother in the bedroom, running a fine seam with the electric sewing machine. She liked her mother as a genuine person—which was a sort of tribute in its way.

She was an efficient, realistic mother for a girl to have, and most of the time a daughter knew exactly what she meant or whether she was angry or glad. But she had a

33

hidden side too. Sometimes she didn't quite get drawers closed or projects finished, and she was nearly always late to appointments. On those occasions, Mr. Long would sit waiting in silence and wearing a relaxed, indulgent smile. What Vada didn't learn until she was practically grown was that he always allowed plenty of time for Mrs. Long to be late in.

The older woman stopped the machine and smiled. She and her daughter were almost the same size except in some fairly subtle details, but they weren't dress-alikes by any means. Mrs. Long had her own appropriate style which never encroached upon girlhood, which with her was past and over, and thank heaven for that.

"Through studying?" she asked pleasantly.

"Uh-huh."

There was a silence. Mrs. Long fiddled with bobbins and bit a couple of threads. That way she was a primitive; other mothers would use scissors. Then she turned questioning eyes, brown like Vada's own.

"Mother—"

"Yes?"

"When did you first meet Daddy? I mean the very first time."

Questions did not disturb Mrs. Long. She thought them all important. "In high school, as I've told you. The first time? We were freshmen, I think."

"Did you—well, did you go steady with him right away?"

The older woman's eyes softened, but her expression didn't change. "My, no," she said. "In fact, the first time we ever went out together was to the senior prom. He—" She smiled.

Apparently, Vada's mother decided not to tell what had happened, but whatever it was still amused her.

"But, Mother—" impetuously, "if you knew him when

34

he was only a freshman, why did it take so much time to—to—"

Mrs. Long became serious. "To bring him to his senses? Well—" She turned and adjusted the tension on the machine a tiny bit. "In those days we didn't start dating quite so early, you know," she finally said. "And— well, I suppose your father just wasn't ready."

"Wasn't ready? What do you mean by that, Mom?" The expression fitted Loren Wallace perfectly. He not only wasn't ready; he was only about half done.

"Exactly that," her mother replied. "Some boys aren't ready as soon as others. They take longer to grow, perhaps because they have a lot more growing to do than others."

"I think I understand," Vada told her. "And thanks."

"By the way," the older woman began, "how's Loren Wal—?"

But her daughter had already gone.

Back in her room, Vada got ready for bed. Her mirror had disclosed a tiny blemish which deserved a frown. But because her mind was on a matter of much more importance, she gave it no heed.

"He isn't ready," she remarked instead. "It could take years."

But before she went to sleep she considered methods for hastening the process a tiny bit, yet there were flaws in every plan. With Loren, almost nothing she could think of seemed to fit the subject. He was so—well, so dense in a nice way that—

For an instant she wondered if that had been her father's trouble. Probably. Perhaps men didn't change from one generation to the next; only women did. And subtly, at that.

CHAPTER 3 . . .

KNOWING THAT Vada Long planned to ac-
celerate his readiness would have shocked Loren, but if
he realized who else worried about him he would have
bleated in terror. It was Miss Terwilliger. Whenever that
mentor began turning her attention to special cases something usually gave, which meant that another good man
got broken.

After bringing Vada home, with appropriate apologies
to her cooperative parents, Lanetta Terwilliger drove to
her tidy apartment on the edge of town. Doing so, she
gunned her foreign sports car a little, and it responded
like a bright freshman.

Darkness had fallen. School board members were safely
within their stuffy houses, loading themselves with starchy
foods and overly rich desserts, no doubt. The teacher had
at least two of them marked for violent heart attacks
before the year was out. The other five members had
been students in her classes. Among a vast array of useful
hints forcefully acquired therein, they knew enough not
to overeat. At least not while she was still in Carleton and
could advise them from day to day.

"Perhaps I'll outlast them all, consolidated or not," she
told herself now, smiling grimly to the road ahead.

Her lasting qualities had been most significant, she

realized at this late hour in the ebb and flow of pedagogical strife. Only Lanetta Terwilliger knew the truth—that she was getting old at last, and tired.

To be sure, the wild spirit to bend the twig and teach it something was still there—if anything, surging ever higher. Yet slowly she had begun to admit that the flesh was weak.

It wasn't the ordinary weakness of those who simply settle and spread. Rather, it was that Miss Terwilliger needed the strength of ten at least, and had once possessed it. Now, as time spelled its inevitable downhill message, she had only the strength of eight or nine, and it wasn't enough.

She pulled expertly into her narrow garage, extracted an enormous briefcase which had been taking up most of the back seat, and went upstairs, where she immediately brewed herself a long cup of tea. It was a special blend imported from friendly tea pastures and had the effect of reviving her quickly. Actually, there was no time to lose. The forces of simian ignorance lurking in the cultural swamp that was Carleton never slept. So neither could she.

As she sipped the invigorating beverage, she planned her dinner. There were some lovely fat carrots and crisp, munchy celery in the refrigerator, carefully wrapped to preserve their essence. And there were plenty of nuts to nibble.

Yet dwelling on her hidden weakness had prompted Miss Terwilliger toward self-indulgence. Tonight she intended to eat a whole can of sardines and even broil a lamb chop. She wasn't a vegetarian at all, but preferred to maintain a balance. A woman did welcome a change now and then from whole grain, safflower products, and sophomores.

"Weakness!" she said aloud fiercely, taking the last sip

37

and automatically reading her fortune in the bottom of the cup.

Her Aunt Charity had taught her how years ago. Charity had visited in Winona for a time when her husband, a sort of American gypsy who sold things while traveling, was on tour. Aunt Charity was the one Terwilliger who had turned out poorly—although Lanetta recalled her, poor soul, as a terribly jolly person, considering the depths of ruined character from which her laughter had to emerge. After Charity had left, the family spent a good deal of time ridding the children of her influence, but telling tea-leaf fortunes was not easily forgotten. Evidently sin had its sly message even for a Terwilliger.

What she saw in her cup tonight held dire portent. There were mud, storm, woeful proceedings, and dark deeds on a murky field. One sign definitely indicated crossed bars, the gallows probably, and departures of known masculine miscreants.

It was all in fun, of course. Nobody could predict the future, especially these days. Idly and with a bemused smile, Miss Terwilliger tried to think of somebody she knew who deserved the gallows. Naturally, from a host of candidates she picked but one, since there was really only one to draw. And quarter.

"Hugh Busch!" she said, letting her tongue pronounce away the whole phonic substance of the syllables as a cat licks up cream.

Then she amended the thought at once, because Mr. Busch was one of her dear colleagues on the staff at Carleton High School. Wishing him the gallows even in jest was not exactly professional. Departure would be enough, of a type used by Mr. Francis Vandermeer last June.

Among other presumed tasks, Mr. Vandermeer had

38

been one Carleton band instructor who should never have been permitted out of the reeds. He came from Florida and immediately sought and found other employment, leaving for Venezuela the day school was out, to the everlasting relief of music lovers and possible local caribou huntsmen.

To catch up the Vandermeer torch, Mr. Hipper had assumed the band duties, conducting it from afar. The principal's theory, apparently, was that a youthful musician should learn his instrument from the inside out— which might work with the drum and tuba. Meanwhile, the board had hired Mr. Busch, who did seem to know the rudiments of science and mathematics but little else. Miss Terwilliger often wondered why the poorest students in a high school always stayed home and got themselves elected to the school board.

Once or twice she had wondered what it was she disliked about Mr. Busch. The school sorely needed a fairly adequate science teacher, and he was that, she could admit. Finally she had to own that her distaste was personal; she deplored his obnoxious personality.

Yet there were reasons. He was one of those youngish-appearing men whom books describe as frail, a small individual of a type she regarded with natural suspicion, she being nearly six feet tall herself. A person could stumble in the teachers' lounge, fall, and crush Busch.

Additionally, he had a number—possibly three—of ill-clad, boisterous children scampering without restraint around the adjacent grammar school. Mrs. Busch was one of those colorless, slender wives who cling to cars, men, doorways, railings, and vacuum cleaners and speak in soft, tiny voices. Thus Busch, being all these things—frail, obnoxious, unskilled, and with family responsibilities far beyond his capacity—should have known his place. He didn't.

Busch was brash; that was the only way to describe the sniggly little man with his insipid hobby of reading barometers and isothermal maps. He irritated Miss Terwilliger more each day. For one thing, of all the men teachers in her memory, Hugh Busch was the first and only one with the temerity to call her by her first name in public. "Hello, Lanetta," he began yipping out in the lounge almost from his first day, which was bad enough. Familiarity around schools was bad practice lest the students follow suit and destroy dignity.

Now, only last week, he had gone even farther in his vulgarian way. "Hi there, Lanny," he had yelled in bull-like tones. As with so many little, little men, nature had tried her best to compensate with Busch. He had a strong, full voice, resonant and rangy, so that she could imagine his vocal cords deep in his throat in a state of disproportionate development greater than his major muscles.

Worse, Mr. Busch was the portrait and prototype of weak, flabby humanity supine. When at rest, he didn't sit up straight as others must; rather, he lay down in a chair, having the physique for such an improbable maneuver.

In class, instead of standing the whole time as good hard-subject teachers knew to be proper, Busch lounged. In the cafeteria, he seemed always at the point of falling asleep, and he yawned frequently whenever someone discussed the fine points of the new, tougher education. Even worse, he had not bothered to attend two important meetings of the teachers' association, of which Lanetta Terwilliger had been everything from president to historian. He was soft.

"I was watching the ball game," he had explained afterward, "and I completely forgot, Lanny. Sorry. Better luck next time."

It was partly because of Mr. Busch that Miss Terwilliger worried about Loren Wallace this year more than last.

40

Although entirely different from the teacher physically, mentally he showed signs of teetering in some sort of Busch balance. As many of the young people liked to put it in their quaint jargon, he was not with it, exactly as Hugh Busch was not. Another of the soft science teacher's revolting habits was to twirl a lock of his hair absently whenever he was trying to think, which was seldom. Lately she had noticed Loren doing the same thing, although the effect was different. Twirling a lock of hair one-half inch long presented problems in logic.

There were other clues. In English class, Loren often looked as if he was falling into hypnotic trance—a typical Buschism if she had ever seen one. He was taking two classes from that permissive mountebank—advanced algebra and physics—so naturally there was an influence.

Once while she was explaining the metrical pattern of certain poems, he had even yawned, making the same mocking gesture of stifling himself that Busch used. It was a covering hand motion, except that it outdid itself so that a viewer fancied the whole arm was being stuffed down a throat. Most disconcerting, and doubtless intended so.

Miss Terwilliger permitted herself no more recreational time. Her tea was gone, and the vision of the future destroyed. She washed and dried the cup and saucer, put them away, and prepared dinner at once, setting out a full service on the table, including candlesticks. After a hard day with the youth, she liked nothing better than to dine by candlelight here in her own cozy hideaway. There was a place in every rounded life for romance—all providing one didn't overdo it.

A warm lassitude, a sense of the grace of fundamental living, settled over her as she saw the gleaming silver and immaculate cloth. She decided to go all the way tonight, so she had two lamb chops and saved the sardines. Then after she had dined, with all things cleared, cleaned, put away, or discarded, she was ready to work.

First she sharpened several red pencils to needle points and drew out a batch of sophomore papers. These she read rapidly, swept along by the thrill of the job, only pausing between every two or three words to slash down the mark. Then she entered grades in her book, a task she always found satisfying with sophomores.

Lately, the state had made a good deal of fuss about no-nonsense teaching—no frills, plenty of hard subjects, and a return to the bedrock fundamentals. Why, she had been teaching that way for years and years, using the same sound, solid methods that had been known for a century or more—the learn-by-failure technique. Now, all over the state, they were adopting something like the Ter-williger method—the grammar, the Latin, the good grind-ing drill, the meaty foreign language, the hour-for-hour homework, the merciless elimination of the unfit, and the close attention to the gifted.

"The gifted!" said Miss Terwilliger aloud, glancing up from a sophomore paper that fairly dripped the blood of correction. She saw a few of them in memory—those rare minds that occasionally appeared. A Vada Long, for ex-ample, a— She had to think harder. A Gordon Chance, who was here a decade or more ago. A—

She caught herself sharply. She had almost spoken a name, and having done so, she began to worry about Loren Wallace all the more. For as Lanetta Terwilliger knew very well, more than once she had the disquieting suspicion as she wrote out his "C" in English that Loren was as gifted as anyone.

For example, one yearly sophomore assignment was to write a poem in class. Most of today's parents were ter-rible poets, and if youngsters took the work home, results were frightful. But she'd had mild success under her direct supervision, although there was always a group of rebels who turned in classic samples such as Teddy Jacoby's.

"One thing I hope gets here real soon," he had written, "is June."

Loren's effort, on the other hand, had disturbed her for days. When she had unscrambled the handwriting, Miss Terwilliger had been forced to sit down and read again. She searched her books of modern poetry to find the one he had copied or paraphrased, because the words had a haunting, mystical quality no high school sophomore ever achieved. Not lately in California, at least.

He had written it himself, and gradually it came into perspective as the naïve, boyish, awkward thing the poem was—about childish matters, the hills and the sky, the ocean and the fog, hawks and wind. And how one day a doe and fawn had crossed the road toward the creek. Nothing at all, really. She'd marked down for spelling, punctuation, and form and given him a "C plus."

Yet ever afterward she had worried far back in her mind—as critics and strong teachers must always do. No conscientious teacher wanted to have one of the last of the poets in her class and fail to recognize him—the way this county had done when John Steinbeck attended one of its schools. So that year she gave the poetry assignment twice, and waited. Sure enough, Loren's poem was fanciful to the point of the ridiculous. It was about a calf named Walter, of all things, who had refused to grow up and behave as other cattle. So he'd run away from home one night and joined the wild, free herds in the hills.

She'd felt reassured. The youth was no more than a nice boy, attractive in a gangling way, and Vada Long seemed very interested in him. But he was no more than that.

Yet now that junior English was at hand, she wasn't so sure again. Not at all. Only last week, while seeming to be in a state of somnambulism, he had grasped the point of literature with sharper insight than even Vada Long. In his tortured prose, seemingly torn with pliers from a ball-point pen and then written by chickens, he had divined the theme and meaning of an especially difficult story and described the style with appalling precision.

This time she had gone to the records. There was nothing to show—that is, except for one galling dissent. At the end of the first quarter, Hugh G. Busch had given Loren two "A's," the first he had ever received in high school.

She sighed. Loren Wallace worried her; no doubt about it.

Work done and the long day over, she retired and slept the sleep of the just about had. Yet in the morning she awoke refreshed and ready for the new day of drill, rote, failure, and learning. There was zest in her step and fire in her eyes as she breakfasted, set the apartment into customary Spartan order, and prepared her unflinching mind for the rigorous day ahead.

But just before leaving for school, where she liked to be ready at least a half hour before any students arrived, she telephoned the office. Little Marjorie Waynright, the secretary, was supposed to be on the job at eight. Miss Terwilliger liked to call once in a while to find out if that was true.

This time it was. "Why, Marjorie, dear," said the teacher, "how nice to hear your cheerful voice this morning! I was wondering if you'd ordered those workbooks for me, as—"

She listened. Marjorie had ordered the books, but she had more important news.

Miss Terwilliger almost dropped the phone. "In the hospital!" she managed after she had caught her breath. "The rest of the semester!"

The receiver buzzed.

44

"Yes, Marjorie. I suppose so, but—there might be another way. We teachers always find one, you know."

She hung up.

A few minutes later she was in her classroom with assignments on the board. The school had to go on through sun and snow and sleet and night, whatever happened. Yet in all her experience, which included boiler breakdown, termite infestation, and new state superintendents, Carleton High School had never had a crisis quite like this one.

Still, she remained calm. She had to. It had been Principal Hipper's decision to have first-period teachers make the fateful announcement. It would be enough for him, he insisted, to answer all the silly questions during the rest of the day. Doubtless the man was closeted in his office right now preparing for the ordeal. John Hipper was the latest in a series of principals, and although his tenure went back a number of years, like the others he was too weak for the post.

The halls filled precipitously, and the merry, inane babble of young voices reached her. Today they were to begin reading *Hamlet,* and the work would go on no matter what. That was the ingredient they needed: work, discipline, and challenge.

Little Sarah Kimberly was first to come inside and take her place as usual. Sarah said, "Good morning, Miss Terwilliger," almost with what could have been a curtsy, given a little deeper knee bend. If all her students could only be like Sarah, she reflected, life would be a good deal simpler.

But they weren't. Thinking about that difference made the teacher's jaw set a little firmer, and her eyes took on more gray—like stainless steel. In a sense, she was glad, deep down, that they weren't all Sarahs. Teaching could lose much of its salt.

Ah—here were two individuals with some of the tang. They bore textbooks with the typical ostentation of those who read slowly and with reluctance.

"Good morning," sang out one in his spurious border twang. "How are you today, Miss Terwilliger? It's nice to—"

"Just sit down," she told Teddy Jacoby. "And you too, Joe. Copy the assignment from the board."

The first bell rang and the whole junior class—or most of it—trooped in. Young Hodges, Vada Long, the Tuthouse scion, and all the rest. They took their places like little soldiers, bright-faced, scrubbed, full to the brim with corn chips and a few other things.

She held her grade book in readiness, to take the roll, to inscribe an "F," or meet any emergency, noticing with satisfaction that only one seat was unfilled. Whatever else Carleton youth might be, it was healthy and active.

Before the second bell stopped ringing, she began the necessary clerical work, frowning and marking the square of the absentee first, noting the name—Loren Wallace.

Then a gray shape slipped into the corner of her vision, found a place, and squatted down. Slowly, Miss Terwilliger erased the mark. Loren wasn't absent; he was late. Tardiness was serious.

As proof of her worry about that lad, she did the exceptional, almost the dramatic, and let him stay without going to the office for an excuse. He would miss the announcement, and it concerned him as much as anyone else. The last time she had overlooked a tardiness was in 1945—for a boy who had torn his pants on the brass eagle of the flagstaff in assembly. It was the unusual.

Her eyes glittered as she snapped the grade book shut. "Class," she said in her high, courageous voice, "Mr. Hipper has asked me to make an important announcement about something I'm sure you'll think very unfortunate."

46

They settled back. Juniors were accustomed to misfortune.

"Coach Blount has influenza," she continued simply.

She saw the Tuthouse youth nod his head, but beyond that there was almost no reaction. Sometimes, in first period, Miss Terwilliger felt like firing off blank cartridges and cracking a whip.

Sarah put up a dimpled hand. "Is the coach very sick? I mean, there's the one-day flu, and the—"

"Two-day," somebody volunteered.

They all looked grave. The two-day, fallout flu could be mighty unpleasant, and nobody wanted to see a good guy like Coach Blount felled that long.

"I'm sorry," went on Miss Terwilliger. "It isn't the regular flu at all; it's more like pneumonia. Coach Blount is very sick and in the hospital. His doctors say that very likely he won't be back for the rest of the seas—"

She noticed that it was Loren's jaw that dropped first and farthest, probably because it was held loosest. But then the expression traversed the entire class and the groan came—one of those collective groans teachers learn to recognize. Afterward, babble broke.

Lanetta Terwilliger knew catastrophe when she saw it coming, but it took her almost a full two minutes to regain control, a record since her first year.

Finally, when only a faint shuffling of restless feet broke the stillness, she said: "That's all I can tell you now about Mr. Blount. Please open your books to the page number I have written on the board, where you can read it over and over again if you must. We come to *Hamlet*, at last. *Hamlet*, boys and girls, is a reading experience you will never forget."

Yes, the work had to go on. In public education, the soft, malleable minds of the youth came first. That before anything else.

CHAPTER 4...

LOREN HAD BEEN LATE for a legitimate reason, namely, that Mr. Busch had delayed him. The Busch family automobile, a classic station wagon more sick than classy, had stalled. Happening along, Loren had obligingly pushed Mr. Busch around the block a few times until the old engine fired.

"You'll probably be late," the teacher had said, thinking ahead in his scientific way while the engine roared. It needed mufflers too. "Here, I'll write you a note."

He'd bent over the hood of the car and scribbled something on a scrap of paper which turned out to be an old unpaid gas bill. Loren had accepted the message with thanks, knowing very well that Miss Terwilliger never would. Stuff scribbled on old gas bills had never been legal tender in that class and might make swift justice worse. Still, by finding a quick parking space at school, running across lawns and a few shortcuts, he'd almost made it.

Luckily she hadn't noticed him. He'd shrunk down into his seat as if nothing had happened, panting so hard that Alice Hodges, who sat next to him, looked as if he was going to administer artificial respiration by using the mouth-to-mouth method. Naturally, Hodges didn't say anything; he knew better than to use words in English class.

The stunning announcement of Coach Blount's disease banished all other thought. Without a coach there could be no team until a substitute was located—which might not be too easy, judging from past substitutes they had brought in around Carleton.

A good share of the team was here, and Loren could tell that people felt a sense of responsibility for having laid the faithful old coach low. A sort of hollow groan went up, especially from Tuthouse. Quite a few accusing glances got sent his direction, because everyone remembered how Lardboy kept the man damp with wet towels.

There was one tiny ray of bright. If Blount was sick before the Paso Verde and Almond Grove games, for the first time in years Carleton would have a good excuse for finishing last in the league. But that didn't leaven the gloom.

Loren reviewed the possibilities quickly. Mr. Hipper had to be counted out. First, he was too busy being principal and teaching band, and secondly, he was opposed to football entirely, especially the eleven-man type. He favored consolidation even though he would lose his own job, and last year he'd gone before the board and tried to have the team abolished.

"It's vain and fantastic," he was reported to have said. "Putting our boys up against a school of Almond Grove's enrollment is dangerous, gentlemen. In a hog-calling contest, the young Carleton men might have a chance, but in football, no." Naturally, the board had overruled him.

That left Mr. Busch as the only man available, and even someone who liked the little science teacher could see it was ridiculous. He might coach a chess squad or a team in competitive magic squares, but out on the Carleton field he'd have to be anchored down with tent stakes to keep him from blowing away. He didn't go over a hundred and ten pounds in his clothes, and everyone in his classes had noticed him turn white from overexertion when he picked up an extra-heavy bundle of paper.

Loren stopped trying to figure solutions. It was a problem for the master planners and out of the scope of mere juniors. He hoped Coach Blount got well fast, but he knew from experience how fallout flu could nail a person.

He began his customary battle to focus a so-called mind on the subject while Miss Terwilliger maintained order. That was easy for her. A person got the idea or else. If he didn't, he would soon reap his fine reward—which was that he took junior English next year at the same time he was taking senior English.

There were always quite a few whimpering seniors around who were doing just that. Merely watching them slink from locker to library for more outside reading was enough. The other alternative was to quit school and join the Navy, and even that great bunch of sea dogs didn't want a kid without a high school diploma. Oh, a few made it, by dropping to their knees in recruiting offices. But not many.

When the usual unearthly silence had settled, everyone whipped open his book to the page and began to read *Hamlet*, with various people taking assigned parts. Miss Terwilliger had the idea that Shakespeare didn't come alive until read aloud and explained phonetically as a student went along.

The first scene was about some soldiers at a castle in Denmark. Loren read the part of a guy named Horatio who was a friend of Hamlet's. He was fairly superstitious and maybe sick, because right away he began seeing ghosts. Down at Almabuena hospital, when a person did that, he knew he wasn't right.

Miss Terwilliger took the ghost part and played it like a veteran. Then Alice Hodges, who was Bernardo, hollered, "What, is Horatio there?"

Loren answered, "A piece of him," which was about the way he felt. Others in class nodded.

The ghost was supposed to look like some dead king who "smote the sledded Polacks on the ice," and with Miss Terwilliger, it figured. Horatio claimed they should all run and tell Hamlet the bad news. Marcellus, who was Lardboy, said he knew exactly where to find Hamlet—which should have been easy because it was dawn and cocks were crowing. Anybody would be in bed grabbing some shut-eye at that hour.

Gradually the class relaxed, probably from learning that Carleton wasn't the only place in trouble. Denmark hadn't been so good either.

Interest picked up in the second scene, which was as far as they got that morning. Hamlet turned out to be this odd character running around in black suits and reciting poetry. He wanted to get back to school in Wittenburg, but his mother, the queen, wouldn't let him do it. Usually, it was the other way around. A fellow's mother made him go to school whether he wanted to or not. There had to be a reason. Sure enough, Hamlet wore black because his father had died. Also, he was a little worried because his mother had married an uncle only a month later— which wasn't the common practice even back then. Not only that, Horatio was also skipping his classes at Wittenburg—which wasn't considered too good an idea at Carleton.

Miss Terwilliger had the class write a short paragraph about what they had learned so far. Everyone picked the story as a murder mystery right away, from seeing so much television. They figured Hamlet's father had been murdered and the uncle was the killer. Why? Because the ghost was a clue. Even the teacher admitted it, but she said they had to read the rest of the play anyhow, because picking the guilty man in the first scene wasn't the point of great literature. According to her, the play was the thing, the same as in football.

Just before the period ended, Mr. Hipper sent around a bulletin announcing that football practice was canceled that afternoon. Then the bell rang and people got sprung from English—which was lucky. Loren figured they knew scientifically that fifty minutes of that subject was all a junior could stand at any one sitting.

During that day, there were as many rumors and portents as ever showed up in Hamlet's time. Every five or ten minutes somebody had a new version. They ran all the way from a new miracle drug bringing the coach back from the brink, to the idea that the team could go coach itself if it wanted to.

All Mr. Hipper would say was that he was trying to get a substitute, but so far no luck. There were plenty of retired teachers of everything from animal husbandry to the fundamentals of knitting, but no football coaches. He had already found a Mrs. Avis Snively to take Mr. Blount's U. S. history classes.

By noon, the whole school regretted the loss, especially boys. Instead of going to regular physical education classes, they had to sit in study hall with Mrs. Snively, who gave them a dandy lesson in hygiene. The combined study hall and library at Carleton was a huge, bare room which dated to times when schools had about eighty kids in each class.

When the last bell rang, Loren and Teddy Jacoby wandered over toward the boys' gym. "Knew something like this was going to happen," Jacoby said.

"How did you know?"

"Easy. Merely psychology. The coach probably wanted to get sick."

"How do you figure?"

"So he could get out of the humility," Teddy said. "Being last in the league is failure, Wallace, and realizing you've failed year after year eats into a man."

Loren shrugged. Could be—except that Blount never had been too humble and by this time he should have been used to losing.

They found a lot of the other fellows milling around the locked doors of the gym—like sheep, Loren thought. Lardboy was yelling that it was probably Almond Grove bacteriological warfare, but Jack Hewston, a guard, took umbrage. Also high dudgeon. In other words, he was mad.

"Yah, Tuthouse," he hollered, "you mean you did it by keeping locker rooms like a swamp all afternoon. Us guys got colds too, on account of all that excess steam you let loose."

"Right," Alice Hodges bellowed, taking sides. "Plaster in the gym is all moldy from Tuthouse steam."

It was a rallying cry, coming that way from Hodges. Pro-Tuthouse and anti-Tuthouse factions quickly formed. Loren's sentiments were with Lardboy, naturally. Why? First because he was a friend, and secondly because the school boilers didn't put out that much hot water. Unless a person got in the showers early enough for the first couple of gallons, the water came out ice-cold.

By that time, Lardboy was glancing around wildly for sympathy, sort of like a cornered rat begging for mercy. But the argument about the cause of Coach Blount's illness might never have been settled if there hadn't been an interruption. As it was, Tuthouse probably would have to carry guilt for life.

"There they are," voices squeaked from across the courtyard. Woman voices.

Loren froze; he recognized one of them. Vada. Also Miss Terwilliger. She was striding across the lawn toward them, surrounded by the staff of the Carleton *Tatler*. Vada, being editor, was at the teacher's right-hand side, naturally,

53

and scampering along behind were some other women such as Shirlee Danforth, Laneva Chaffee, and Donna Reeder. They were buddies of Vada's and cut of the same stripe, except in different sizes and shapes. Ordinarily, they chattered around like a clutch of nutty sparrows, but in the presence of their awesome leader they were fairly quiet.

They came charging over and took a stance below the gym steps. "You see, girls," Miss Terwilliger gestured with a sweep of her bony hand, "the boys have come out here like so many little sheep who have lost their master. It means—"

Loren noticed that Vada Long wasn't staring at the team; she was looking at him hard, and he could almost feel the wool growing on his back. "Bah," he whispered to himself.

"It means—" Vada said, "that the team—"

"—must go on," finished Miss Terwilliger.

The other women were nodding their cute heads; they thought so too.

"Hasn't Carleton always had a football team to finish out the season, Miss Terwilliger?" asked Laneva in her sweet little voice, way up there in high frequency sound like a surgeon's knife.

"Indeed it has," replied the educator in a stout voice. "If we don't finish this season, it would be the first time in school history. Should that happen?"

"No," cried Donna Reeder fiercely, clenching a small fist tightly. Back in freshman days when Donna had gone steady for about a week with Alice Hodges, she'd used that fist on him to express how she cared. Plenty of people thought it was what had given Hodges his current attitude toward women.

"The team has to go on," Shirlee added in her deep contralto. "Doesn't it, Miss Terwilliger? So what will we do?"

"Don't worry, girls," the teacher assured them, sort of

flinging back her head. "I've already proposed a plan to the board. They're meeting tonight, and we'll know in the morning whether they will be sensible. Now you girls run back and write your story. Vada, can you think of a working idea, like—?"

Vada took one more look at Loren. "How's this?" she said. "Lonely team mopes on locker room steps; waits for sick coach!"

"Splendid!" said Miss Terwilliger. "Wonderful!" She turned to Lavena, who was carrying the school Graflex. "Now hold it right there, boys. All right, Lavena. Take one."

Before anybody could move, Lavena had snapped the shutter.

"All right," the teacher said. "That's all. And, team, you'll know before another night is over how loyalty and spirit is rewarded. I'll see to that."

They left. The Carleton team watched them go with a kind of frigid immobility—as if they had been caught in unspeakable mischief in a dream.

"I knew we'd have trouble," Jacoby said darkly. "I could tell by the signs."

This time even Joe Martinez believed him. "What did she mean, we'll get rewards?" he asked the gods. "I've been rewarded in English a few times. Don't want the same in football, man."

"Here either," agreed Lardboy, shuddering. "Oh, me and my wet towels! Why did I do it?"

"Yeah, why?" Hodges sneered. "Go wave them wet towels of yours at Mrs. Snively, Tuthouse. Or give Ol' Lady Terwilliger pneumonia. Do some good; don't do no more harm."

They stuck around a little while longer, until Mr. Hipper came out and made motions to go away, which they did.

Tuthouse had his car here, so Hodges and Martinez rode

home with Lardboy while Jacoby stayed with Loren. He swung his long, loose frame into the front seat with a kind of melancholy dejection.

"Recall what Hodges said about Vada being out with Bobby Morgan?" he asked.

Loren nodded. He remembered, all right.

"Saw her myself last night," Teddy admitted. "She was rodding around with Bobby and some ugly redheaded woman."

Silence.

"You ought to see Morgan's car," the guy went on, running a finger over a couple of rusty spots on the dashboard of this heap. "Neat? Man, is that a bomb! You ought to notice the custom chrome job he's got. Full chrome wheels, and—"

Loren spun the starter to drown out words, but no use.

"Vada looked real good in Morgan's rod, Wallace," Teddy continued. "That maroon metallic finish sets her off like a jewel, and—Well, you should see the thin-line whitewalls, and—"

Loren churned out of there, ignoring a buddy, and Jacoby must have got the idea, because he was quiet for a few blocks. Finally, they reached his place, a white frame house on a corner.

"Thanks," he said, getting out like a ruler unfolding. "Oh, and by the way, know what Morgan said to me about the game?"

"No."

"Said that this year the score against us was going to be a hundred to nothing, sure. But he doubted he'd even get to play. Claimed the Almond Grove coach plans to use their fourth string the whole time."

"He said that?"

"Yeah. And do you know what?"

"No."

"I believe him—although I doubt we can keep the score that low with Blount gone. Maybe it would be better if we dropped football. Got in enough time for a varsity letter?"

"No."

"Neither have I," said Jacoby. "But maybe us Carleton guys shouldn't have letters. Could be we deserve numbers or something. Well, thanks for the ride, Loren, although—" He tapped the hood of the car with a probing hand. "You've got a strange engine under there. What is it, a V-two-and-a-half? Sounds like it."

Teddy went into his house and Loren took off. It was good to have a buddy like that—always trying to be helpful. He got the picture of Vada riding in Morgan's convertible, and he had to admit she belonged there. No girl with her style would ever ride in a heap like this one, and Jacoby was merely trying to tell him that—in a nice way.

His friendship was demonstrated again later that evening. About ten, Loren's mother called him to the telephone. It was Teddy.

"Know Hodges?" he asked.

Who didn't?

"Know his dad is president of the school board?"

"Sure."

"Well, Hodges says his dad just got back from an emergency meeting. They made a decision about the team."

Loren thought that over. It had to come, he supposed. They'd probably decided to withdraw for the rest of the schedule. Maybe forever.

"We turn out for practice tomorrow," Jacoby said.

"We do? Who's the new coach?"

"Dunno," Jacoby said. "That's why I called you, Wallace. It's peculiar. Hodges wouldn't tell me. All he'd say was that his dad came home from board meeting looking as if he'd seen a ghost or something—"

"A ghost! There aren't any such—"

"I said, 'or something,' Loren," Teddy explained tiredly. "Hodges figured maybe his dad had seen a monster. Plenty of monsters around these days. All he'd say was that we'd find out the truth soon enough, and no use to ruin a night's sleep for everyone in town." Jacoby paused. "Well— merely wanted to tell you. Knew you were anxious, Wallace, and I wanted to calm you down."

A pal like that would always think of others before himself. "Thanks," Loren said. "It's a big help."

CHAPTER 5...

LOREN HAD NATURAL CURIOSITY. He got to school a good half hour early the next morning to learn who was the new Carleton coach.

Almost the whole team was there already. A few of them—the excitable type like Bugatti, Hewston, Hodges, and some others—were waving their arms. Gesticulating, Miss Terwilliger would call it. Others of the more thoughtful, cowardly type were standing dead still with expressions of shocked disbelief on their faces. Loren noticed especially the stunned-fish look of both Jacoby and Tuthouse; on them the news had hit bone. Teddy seemed to twitch, whereas Lardboy had gone rigid.

Meanwhile a kind of rabbity shadow passed in and out among the large shapes of team members. It was Mr. Busch; he spoke to various ones and tried to soothe them.

Loren got to Tuthouse first, because he was on the outskirts of the mob. "What happened, Lardboy?" he asked gently, so as not to awaken him too much. He'd heard that waking people from catatonic spells was dangerous; from then on they would very likely go entirely daft. Yet with Tuthouse, people might not notice too much difference.

Sure enough, Lardboy came to with a horrid jerk, and his eyes swam around awhile, out of focus.

"Happened?" he asked in a pathetic, scared voice.

"Yes. What's going on?"

Lardboy suddenly began to giggle; the noise was pretty gruesome. It was like these ghoulish sounds from the grave, the same as in *Hamlet,* where Horatio claimed the sheeted dead did squeak and gibber in the Roman streets. Tuthouse had a real gibber on him.

"We—we just found out."

"What? What did you find out, Lardboy?"

The guy groaned again and dropped hands to sides in a gesture of despair. "Who the new coaches are, Wallace," he jabbered. "We know now, and—"

By that time Hodges and Jacoby had come up.

"What's the matter with Lardboy?" Loren inquired. "Is he sick?"

"No," said Teddy. "He's not sick. Not yet, anyhow. You sick, Tuthouse? I mean, physically?"

"Who are the new coaches, Teddy?" Somehow that information tied up with this scene.

Jacoby cocked his head. "You spoke, Wallace?" he whispered. "You asked a question such as who are the new coaches?"

"Sure. Why not?"

Teddy took a deep swallow of air. "I cannot tell a falsehood," he said, "especially to a true friend. Loren, the new coaches are—" He gulped again, hesitating.

"Go on, tell him," Alice Hodges grunted, poking Jacoby with a stout-headed thumb. "Why should Wallace get spared? He ain't no better than the rest of us."

Teddy opened his mouth so his teeth hung out fine, and his tongue got poised for dandy plosive sounds. But nothing came out; only a kind of choked-up gargle.

"I c-c-can't," he finally stuttered. "H-Hodges, I honestly c-can't. There's something about those s-syllables I can't speak."

60

Alice Hodges snorted, and the muscles of his size-seventeen neck bunched a little. "Might have guessed it," he sneered. "Jacoby, all you do is talk, talk, talk when the going is smooth. But in a clutch, you ain't able to speak. If you can't talk, what can you do?"

"Nothing," ruefully. "Guys, I'm no good. I'm—"

"Oh, man!" Hodges growled. "Loren, you're goin' to find out anyhow, so you might as well get that there news from a friend. The new coaches are Mr. Busch, and—"

"Mr. Busch!" yelped Loren, aghast at what a board of education could do in those star-chamber sessions when no honest citizen was awake. "You mean he's going to train us how to defend ourselves from those Almond Grove gorillas?" He blanched, which was what happened to an almond when the heat was on.

"Wait!" Hodges commanded, raising a paw. "You think Busch is bad, huh, Wallace? You intimate fine old Busch ain't goin' to be satisfactory compared to—"

"—to who's the other coach," Teddy Jacoby said.

Alice gave him the baleful eye. "Yeah. Like I said, compared to who's the other coach—"

There was a silence, broken only by crowd mutterings.

"Well," Loren asked, "let's have it. Who is he?"

"He—" Hodges laid a kindly arm on a pal's shoulder. "He? Wallace, old buddy, Busch is only assistant coach. His job is to watch locker rooms for we guys an' pick up wet Tuthouse towels. The head coach, that there wily mentor us guys need to take over until Blount gets back is—is none other—than—than—"

"Say it," Jacoby insisted. "Go on, Hodges. You tell Loren the facts. Say the name—"

"Keep quiet!" Alice snarled fiercely. "Was gonna until you busted in. Hadda take a breath is all, because—"

"Say it! Roll it around on your tongue. Think of us football heroes and the reports of games in newspapers. Read in your imagination the headline, 'Carleton team, coached by—' "

"Cut that there out!" Hodges pleaded. "Stop that psychological suggestion you're always trying, Jacoby. I can say the name; saying it don't bother me none. It's—it's—"

"Miss Terwilliger," butted in Tuthouse. He was the only one with the raw intellectual courage. "She's the new head coach, Loren. What's so unusual about that? I mean, in an emergency such as we've got, who else would they pick? What other teacher around here has the qualifications—the brain, the brawn, the—?"

"Nobody," admitted Loren, not realizing what he was saying. "She's the right man for the—" He felt paralysis coming on. "Huh?" he managed to gasp before it got him. "Miss Terwilliger—our coach. No!"

"Yeah!" said Alice Hodges.

Loren didn't begin to thaw and get back to reality until third period. Then he recalled that someone in English class, Sarah Kimberly, maybe, had asked Miss Terwilliger if that was what her students were supposed to call her from now on: "Coach."

"No, Sarah," the teacher had said. "I'd prefer that you continued to call me by my regular title. Neither Mr. Busch nor I is really a coach. We're simply going to take charge at football practice and supervise it like a regular academic class. Mr. Blount will keep in touch and outline a day's work until he returns. So I'm not the coach, Sarah. I am only a loyal Carleton teacher who doesn't want the team to disintegrate. Do you understand?"

Sarah understood, but nobody else did. As Loren got it, he was the only man on the squad who hadn't decided to turn in his suit this afternoon. Football was glorious, sure, but most of them didn't want the glory quite that much.

"Also it's dangerous," Hewston claimed. "Suppose somebody busts a spine in scrimmage this afternoon. Coach

Blount would merely tape it up and we'd be safe. But out there with Busch and Miss Terwilliger calling the signals, why—"

He made a popping noise with his tongue, which was like a backbone snapping. The poor fellow would go through life with a fatally fractured skeleton.

"Did you notice the women around this fair school?" Vic Morningstar added. "I have. I caught my girl of the hour, Helen Dolan, really snickering because we had a woman coach. A Terwilliger-type woman, at that."

Hewston stepped in and laid a heavy arm on Vic, who stopped the yak right there. Nobody went on talking when Hewston asked for silence; he had barbell muscles. "Which hour exactly was it, Morningstar?" he suggested.

"Don't know what you mean," Vic said.

"I mean when Helen Dolan was your woman. Was it just this past hour, the way I think it was, or you got a future?"

Morningstar happened to remember that Helen was one of the few girls with whom Hewston went steady. "No special hour," he said. "I was just talking with her. You know how it is with me. Any woman I talk with I call a girl of the hour. Merely an expression."

"Naturally," said Hewston, taking down the arm.

By that time, Alice Hodges had begun to comprehend Vic's message. "He meant that the crazy women are laughing at us, was all. So if them stupid females get amusement, think how that there league is going to take it. Guys, we'll never live it down. Fifty years from now if we mention we went to Carleton High—and we gotta on military applications and stuff—people will remember. You know, same way they recall the guy who run the wrong way in the Rose Bowl."

"They'll say we were the team coached by a English teacher," Sam Ritchie added. "That's even worse."

"They'll call us names in public prints," somebody in the rear yipped. "The—the ponytails, or the—the petticoats, or—"

"Knock that there off," Hodges declared. Nobody's going to call us no friendly names like ponytails or petticoats. Why? I'll tell you why. Any of you guys took a good look at Ol' Lady Terwilliger lately, like in the last week?"

Heads nodded no. Only so much a person wanted his tender young eyes to see.

"Well, I have," Hodges said dourly, "on account of I got to look at her because there ain't no obstructions between me and her in English class. It's the angle of my desk. Guys, they'll call us Bloomer Boomers, or something like that."

People thought that over. "Bloomers?" a freshman-type voice wanted to know. "What's bloomers? Never heard of them."

"Me either," Hodges admitted. "Then I seen some old college annuals my mom has. Men, bloomers is a sort of baggy-style pants made outta umbrella cloth. Women wore 'em in olden times."

"Why?"

"Who knows?" said Alice. "But my dad says Miss Terwilliger went to Winona State Teachers College and starred in sports. Field hockey, soccer, basketball, maybe swimming. Well, in them days women wore bloomer things to be on teams, and I'll bet she still does. We go out tonight and there she'll be in them umbrella pants. Somebody from the Almond Grove *Informer* is sure to be around. So we'll get tabbed as Bloomers, sure!"

"I quit," Sorenson said. He'd been quiet up until then.

With Sorenson gone, the captain and star fullback, others gave up. So that was that.

Quitting in midstream was not the Wallace way. Except for Billy Dade, who was so uncoordinated he had to

64

walk sideways to go forward, that left a true one-man squad, namely him—Loren. He'd have to turn out this afternoon all by himself.

"Where's the team?" Miss Terwilliger would likely ask, waving a bloomer or two at him.

"I'm it," Loren would tell her. "Everybody else quit."

"Then get in there and fight," that teacher would command. If there was anyone who would never give up merely because she had only one player on her team, it was Coach Lanetta Terwilliger.

As the day wore on, the story of what had happened gradually emerged. At the emergency meeting last night, Mr. Hipper had claimed he'd scoured the county for a substitute coach who also had a teaching credential. One who did was down with fallout flu himself, which was getting to be an epidemic. Since nobody was available, it was the principal's idea that the rest of the schedule could be dropped with honor.

The board had nodded their heads; because Carleton was already in last place and sure to stay, the team's showing couldn't hurt business much. Also, a couple of members thought that a little studying instead of practice might be good for certain players.

They had been ready to cancel the schedule when Miss Terwilliger showed up. She'd given them an inspiring lecture. For example, she recalled how Mr. Vernon Hewston had captained a team which stood off Almond Grove on the 1-yard line. She mentioned how Mr. Milt Kimberly, when but a sophomore, had scooped up an Almond Grove fumble and run eighty yards for a touchdown. Then she dwelt briefly on how Mr. John Negranti and Mr. Howard Parsons had barely made it through high school because they hadn't turned in senior English themes. Only through Terwilliger intercession had they got their diplomas at all.

As she'd talked, a sort of glassy-eyed fixation had come

over the few spineless types who happened to hold the majority vote. They'd remembered their nickname for her —"Tiger" Terwilliger.

"Now, boys," "Tiger" Terwilliger had said, "here's my idea."

It turned out that she held one of the last unlimited life credentials issued in the State of California—which meant she could teach anything the board authorized.

"And, technically, that would include physical education, wouldn't it? Boys or girls."

Mr. Hipper had admitted it was true, but he doubted that any board of education still in its right mind would be that silly.

"But this isn't just *any* school board, Mr. Hipper," she'd insisted. "This"—pointing around the room—"is the Carleton board!"

It was her idea that she'd merely supervise the boys "at play," as she called it, and when somebody brought up the locker room issue, she had an answer worked out for that too. Mr. Hipper could supervise there, "and rest from his arduous day," as Miss Terwilliger put it. The principal had jumped up and announced he would be blasted if he would; he'd resign first. Two board members had tried to resign right then, but the others wouldn't let them do it.

"Why not draft Busch?" somebody suggested. "As a compromise?"

Miss Terwilliger hadn't wanted that much compromise, but Mr. Hipper claimed that if she had her way on this nonsensical stunt, she took Busch, like it or not, as assistant coach. He'd said that any way this turned out, it would probably go down in educational annals, next to a couple of other things here in California, as the biggest stroke of idiocy since McCarthy shot a hole in the rowboat.

The vote had been taken, and sure enough the count was four to three in favor of Miss Terwilliger's plan. Until Blount got better, she was head coach.

66

Well, it merely meant that Jacoby was right. The wiser heads had flipped. Yet if everyone on the team except the second-string fullback had quit, there wouldn't be much need to worry about Miss Terwilliger's coaching skill.

Plenty of people told Loren that he was a traitor for not making it unanimous. When the last bell rang, he met Jacoby in the hall, and even a buddy was accusing.

"You still going to stay with the team and get coached by—by her?" Teddy asked.

Loren didn't answer. It was no use to try explaining that a Wallace never quit. As with Walter—the family had stuck with that calf through thin and thick; it was Walter who had betrayed.

"Thought so," Teddy said. "Well, see you on the 50-yard line, Wallace. You can center the ball, block the tacklers, throw yourself a pass and be a hero all you want." He took a couple of steps away. "Keep your delusions of grandeur," he added. "So long."

Loren watched him go—a lost friend, at a time when he needed a buddy the most. But that was life; merely miserable.

"Hi, Loren," somebody behind him said. A girl.

He turned around slowly, ready to take their slings and arrows of outrageous fortune, as Shakespeare said. Let them shoot him any style they liked, in the back, or— He blinked.

Sure enough, he knew her. Vada Long. She was staring at him in a mocking manner. She'd probably heard too.

"I think it's—brave, and—and fine of you, Loren," she said.

Taunts. He expected that. But no use to just stand here and let them close in for the kill. A guy had to talk fast and keep ahead of them all the time. "Uh—" he said, making the suave comeback. "Exactly what is?"

"Staying with the team even though the rest quit," Vada said. "Oh, I know it seems funny to boys to be coached by

Miss Terwilliger. Even girls would— But never mind. I admire you, Loren, for sticking it out when—"

He got it; she admired him for being that kind of stupid. It was typical of women. In one fellow, they hankered after his bat-wing ears. In another, skull-bone massiveness rated their plaudits. "Thanks," he told her gruffly, "and many more of them."

"You've saved the after-game dance too," she went on softly. "I was just writing about it for the *Tatler*. If there wasn't a team, there couldn't be a game, so—" She giggled. On her a giggle came out as lovely, whereas on others it wasn't so fine. "So if there wasn't a game, there couldn't be an after-game dance, c-could there?"

He thought that over. It figured. He liked a woman who could use logic. Most of them used everything else but common sense.

"No," he told her. Somehow they had begun walking together toward the office, which was the journalism room. Reflex action, maybe.

"Are—are you going, Loren?" she asked suddenly.

"I'm not sure. Where?"

She turned her head away for a second. Then she came back, smiling faintly. "To the after-game dance. You know, the—the dance after the Paso Verde game."

"Oh, that," he replied in a lonesome, hollow voice.

Loren got a picture of the ecstasy. The Carleton team, which is L. Wallace coached by Bloomer-woman Terwilliger, finishes the game with Paso Verde. All night long, north-county ape-men have pummeled the one-man team, or human football as they playfully call him in the line. The score is a thousand to nothing.

Remaining now is only the dance. Wallace jigs around a few hours on a broken skeletal structure while the orchestra sobs out the fever beat. Happiness.

"Would you want to?" he asked, meaning how could anyone dance in that shape. Dead.

68

She gave a little gasp. "Oh, I'd love to go to the after-game dance with you, Loren," Vada told him, stopping beside a door. "And thank you, thank you ever so much. Well, here I am. I'll see you out on the field this afternoon, Loren. Practicing—"

"You're—going to watch?" he gulped.

"Of course," gaily. "Everybody will be there. It's—it's news, sort of. I don't think there's another high school in the whole country that has a woman English teacher as head coach. Well, good-by, Loren. Don't forget the dance."

She was gone.

"Don't forget the dance," he intoned to himself. Now he grasped implications. In some crazy style, he'd blundered along, taking advantage. Vada thought he'd asked her to go to the dance, and she'd accepted. She'd been too nice and innocent to say no to a traitor like him.

"Agh!" he had to remark. It summed up everything.

He got going again and allowed his feet to chuff him along the hallways toward the gym. But there was no hurry. With only one man on the squad, he probably wouldn't be late for scrimmage.

The first thing he saw when he got inside the locker rooms was Mr. Busch sitting within the glassed-in office. The little science teacher was absorbed in a book, and he twirled a hunk of his hair absently. Concentration.

But that wasn't what got Loren. As his vision grew accustomed to the murky interior, he saw that the whole place was full of the guys in various stages of dress. They weren't hollering and joking around the way they did ordinarily. Instead they were as silent as a television set with a broken picture tube.

Loren felt hushed himself as he picked a careful way through shoulder pads and stuff. Jacoby was there, sitting on the bench, lacing shoes.

"I thought you quit?" he asked Teddy.

"I did," the tall kid nodded, glancing up with a face that showed travail. Jacoby had aged. "I told her."

"What happened?"

Teddy's broad shoulders sort of trembled. He'd got a stoop in about the last half hour. "Wallace," he asked pitifully, "ever take junior and senior English at the same time? No? Ever go from reading *Hamlet* in one class right into reading *Twelfth Night* in another? You didn't? Ever write a junior-type theme and follow it up immediately with a senior-type?"

Loren didn't answer, because why should he? Instead he put his books into a locker and began to suit up as fast as possible.

"And they call this a free country," Jacoby muttered. "No wonder all those guys are out at Almabuena hospital. They probably just wanted to get away from Terwilliger-style freedom."

"I guess," Loren told him in a kindly style.

"You don't guess, Wallace," Jacoby said. "You gotta see it to believe. Hodges was right."

"How so?"

Teddy laughed wildly, but the only sound that came out was a kind of hakk-hakk-hakk.

"Bloomers," he whispered in a scary way. "The crazy bloomers, Loren. And—and a baseball cap. I saw 'em myself!" Then, "Agh-h-h!" said Jacoby, whimpering at last as his spirit broke and he flipped.

70

CHAPTER 6...

IT WASN'T TRUE that Miss Terwilliger wore
bloomers, as subsequent research proved when Loren's
mother described the true article to her son. Instead, these
were a sort of split T formation skirt combined with some
of the qualities of shorts.

Plenty of the guys would have preferred bloomers, even
so. As Alice Hodges put it: "Give me them bloomers any
day. Bloomers is definite."

That first afternoon, youths who were suited up first
didn't charge out on the field but instead bunched inside
the door like hysterical turkeys. Finally, Mr. Busch came
out of the office.

Loren noticed that he had the same faraway look in his
eyes that came over him when he worked a big math problem. He had on a coat Loren liked, one with big patches
of leather on the elbows.

"All right, men," he said in his surprisingly big voice.
"Time to get out on the field."

"Do we have to?" Sam Ritchie asked.

Mr. Busch smiled. "I'm afraid so," he said sympathetically. "There seems no other way."

He had mild blue eyes with a twinkle in them, and was
patient in explaining math processes to those who didn't
grasp them right away. Maybe he liked math and science

himself and wanted others to understand them too—instead of pretending it was this big mystery for a few giant brains to grab.

Nobody had moved; Busch wasn't much of a disciplinarian.

"Mr. Busch," Morningstar said through a plastic helmet. "Can't you—uh—teach football?"

"No," replied the science teacher, "I can't. I don't know anything about being a coach and I didn't play when I was in school. I've watched a few games, but—"

"Then how can Ol', or rather, Miss Terwilliger be our coach?" Hewston wanted to know.

Mr. Busch shrugged. "I don't know. But, boys, if she says she can, the chances are strong that she means it. Miss Terwilliger is"—he hunted around for a right word —"very talented."

"Yeah!" Alice Hodges muttered. "No kidding."

"So please get on out there now, boys," Busch said, "before she—ah—comes in here looking for you. And—uh—give it your best. Give it a try, anyway. In science, you know, we try almost anything in order to—" He brightened. "Perhaps Coach Blount will be well soon. Wonder drugs—uh—do wonders, you know."

"Come on, guys," Sorenson said, because he was captain after all, "let's get there and face it."

Facing it wasn't easy. The sight of Miss Terwilliger in a baseball cap even from this distance could turn back weaklings. She was out in the middle of the field, blowing a few shrill blasts on her whistle and motioning like a sea otter killing fish.

But that wasn't the worst. Lining the field all around were spectators, girls mainly, with a few adults sprinkled in.

"There's Helen Dolan," Morningstar said. "Hey, Hewston, there's your woman."

72

Loren looked that way, but he couldn't see Vada anywhere. Now Miss Terwilliger made more gestures, and the
girls on the sidelines broke into little screams of encour-
agement. Guys in the lead reluctantly got the message, the
same as in English class, and broke into a beefy jog in that
direction until the whole squad was doing it. Finally,
everyone had reached the coach. They huddled there in
front of her, trying to keep a wide buddy between them
and the crowd so as not to be recognized.

Jacoby was behind Loren. "Notice the man on the 50-
yard line," he hissed in a low tone.

"Yes."

"It's Cunningham of the Almond Grove *Informer.*
Sports writer. Man, this must be big news."

A few other characters had begun talking, the way a
youth will do when he is out in open air.

"Silence!" The voice cut out over everyone's head in a
tone that could command armies and sink ships, probably.
Coach Terwilliger had spoken.

She got her wish. They didn't want to take that rawhide
whip twice.

"That's better," said the coach. "Now this afternoon,
boys, the first and second teams will scrimmage. I want
you second-string men to give this all you have. Break up
their plays; charge in hard and rush the passer. Get past
their blockers and bring down their ballcarriers. Teddy
Jacoby, you're acting captain of the second team. Frank
Sorenson, you captain the first team as usual. Now warm
up your men. Play will start when I blow the whistle."

For a second, nobody moved.

"All right," Coach Terwilliger snapped. "Get moving.
Shake the—or, rather—go to your respective ends of the
field. The second team plays for the north goal."

The squad split and did as directed. At the south end,
Jacoby's bunch warmed up by tossing passes and running

73

out under them. Every so often a player would glance out to midfield to see if Coach Terwilliger was still there or if he was merely having a bad nightmare. But no, she was for real.

"If that's womanhood, what am I doing here?" Jacoby asked.

Nobody answered; they didn't know either.

After about five minutes, the whistle blasted and Coach Terwilliger put the ball into play, the first string kicking off. It was Loren's luck that he received. Sorenson tackled him while he was still deciding which way to run—maybe toward home.

Staring up from where somebody had shoved his head into about an inch of ground, he caught sight of Coach Terwilliger's bony knees galloping up. She grabbed the ball and touched it down for the next play.

"Loren," she snapped, "you had the ball in plenty of time to have spun away from Sorenson. Get some go, go, go or you'll take root."

He pulled his face out of the reddish dirt. "All right, Miss Terwilliger."

"Coach Terwilliger," she corrected.

"O. K., Coach," Loren said humbly.

He understood now. She was going to use the same brutal methods to inspire the Carleton team that she used in junior English, and who knew what that would do to the game. Others seemed to be getting the same impression, because the scrimmage got fiercer than usual, with lifetime buddies trying to get up and take various arms and legs that weren't theirs with them. The play seesawed up and down the field with nobody scoring.

Finally, after a series of line bucks, Sorenson threw a pass to Alice Hodges, who ran in broken field and scored. Loren was playing deep, but missed the tackle. He got up slowly and noticed that women on the sidelines were jumping up and down and clapping. He glanced toward the coach; she was doing the same thing. It was fairly horrible.

"Agh!" he said for the second time that day.

"Me too!" Teddy Jacoby exclaimed. "Agh, and double agh!"

Only the failing light of day ended practice, which was another difference from Coach Blount's technique. He liked to get home in time for supper himself.

The guys were genuinely subdued, not even looking at each other, but getting dressed and leaving as quickly as possible. Lardboy Tuthouse only used about a gallon of hot water, and he didn't throw a single towel on the floor for others to pick up after him.

Mr. Busch was going to be some good after all. Maybe he couldn't coach football, but he was a true wizard at first aid. He tied up at least one sprained finger and taped four or five wrenched ankles and wrists like a real professional. So there was no need for Carleton men to lick wounds; not by themselves, at least.

Riding home with Loren, Hodges did blat out once when they hit a rough spot in the road. "Watch it, pencilneck," he yelped. "A guy's got only one spine to lose."

"Sorry," Loren told him.

One by one, he let them out to go limping into their houses. All they said was, "So long," except for Joe Martinez, who kept grinning the whole time but didn't say anything at all.

Teddy was last. "Wallace," he grunted, "know what I think? I mean, about this Terwilliger turn of events?"

"No."

"Neither do I," Jacoby said. "I guess all a person could do to escape is run away. But somebody'd just find you and drag you back."

"I guess," Loren agreed.

English the next day was mainly good advice to a youth. Vada Long read Ophelia's part in the play. Hamlet liked her and she liked him back, but her brother, Laertes, kept warning her not to fall for someone who had to carry Denmark around on his back. Then their fine old father, Polonius, came in and gave Laertes a lot of good advice too, because he was going to Paris. Laertes was supposed to hang on to true buddies, keep quiet and listen, stop borrowing money all the time, and be honest with himself. Wise words. Also Polonius told Ophelia that young love had more light than heat in it and to keep away from Hamlet.

Loren noticed that most football players in the room didn't get too much out of the lesson. They kept eyes glued to the page and didn't look up.

He knew why. She was back to being her regular self with gray hair neat and wearing upswept reading glasses. But every time he looked she'd swim out of focus and he'd see her again in that baseball cap. "Back up that line, Tuthouse!" he'd hear her screaming. "No! No! Hit him down around the knees; let go of his neck. Don't you know how to tackle yet?"

Well, having an English teacher who did know how to tackle was going to make a difference in a student's appreciation of Shakespeare. It could wreck a guy's love of literature, no matter what those hard-subject master planners claimed.

Practice that afternoon was even tougher than before. Coach Terwilliger had everyone running through defensive drills until he was practically beaten down into a pulp. She worked especially on filtering through the line to break up a tricky reverse that Paso Verde liked to use.

Afterward, Mr. Hipper dropped into the locker rooms to see Mr. Busch. Loren, who was dressed, heard them talking inside the office.

"Odd, isn't it?" Mr. Hipper said. He was a tall man, bald on top, with the quizzical expression of someone who has just swallowed an explorer fly.

"Peculiar," Mr. Busch admitted.

"It's—it's so quiet," the principal went on, staring bleakly into the locker rooms. "Seems unnatural." He turned back. "I've been getting phone calls. Surprisingly few complaints. Most townspeople seem to think she should have been head coach all along."

"I—" Mr. Busch began. Then both men noticed Loren and stopped talking.

"No need to tell me, Busch," Mr. Hipper exclaimed. "I think I understand."

He walked out, shaking his head. As he passed Loren, he said: "Hello, Wallace. How's the—ah—the team getting along?"

Loren had to gulp. "To thine own self be true," Polonius had told Laertes, "And it must follow, as the night the day, Thou canst not then be false to any man."

"Uh—" he ventured.

The principal nodded. "Uh!" he repeated. "Yes, I presume the team is in that shape." He left without saying another word.

At that, team morale did sink fairly low. That evening, the Almond Grove *Informer* came out with the story about Coach Blount's duties being taken over by Miss Terwilliger. But instead of making a joke about it, the tone was mighty serious.

The front-page story linked it with the failure of school bonds all over the state, the trend toward tough-subject-style economy, and eliminating the bad apples from classes. It claimed that among needed changes in California education, besides getting farther back to the three R's, the small independent high school district definitely had to go. Carleton's consolidation with Almond Grove

77

was as inevitable as rain. It was time for petty sectionalism and selfish interest to give up. A female football coach was only an example of stubborn provincialism hanging on to frills in a day when the space age demanded bedrock fundamentals and a dollar's worth of learning for a dollar in taxes.

On Thursday, Lardboy Tuthouse had some worse news. "We play Paso Verde tomorrow night, don't we, Wallace?" he asked.

"Yes."

"Well, Sorenson and Morningstar have both come down with the fallout flu. That's what Alice Hodges claims his dad says. Mrs. Morningstar blames Mr. Hodges, on account of he's president of the school board."

It worried certain team members, but Miss Terwilliger didn't seem bothered at all. In English, they read another scene where everyone was at a party, but Hamlet was outside looking for ghosts. Finally, the ghost showed up and took Hamlet for a walk. Then Marcellus, who was Jacoby, said there was something rotten in the state of Denmark. The teacher remarked that it was a famous line that had lived through the centuries, mainly because it described bad conditions almost anywhere.

Finally, Friday night got there. The team was in the locker rooms, with Mr. Busch at his post in the office. An air of gloom hung over the place like fog.

"Wonder who's going to give us the pep talk between halves?" Tuthouse whispered, which was the way they had taken to speaking. "Busch, or Miss Terwilliger?"

People glanced toward the science teacher. He was teetering back and forth in his chair and twirling a hunk of his haircut.

"Not Busch," Alice Hodges said, low in a throat.

Loren noticed how Lardboy had aged in just one week so that he looked at least seventeen. Also Hodges showed the strain; he'd lost plenty of weight here lately—at least a couple of pounds.

"Maybe they both will," he suggested as a compromise. "Us guys can't get too much pep. We could use some."

And that was truth. Out on the field, he saw that Paso Verde was there in full force, overflowing the bleachers. They had their red-and-white pompons solidly massed, and a band that looked bigger than the whole Carleton student body. But that was an optical illusion, probably. Tubas and stuff took up plenty of room.

A roar of good healthy laughs rose from the crowd when the stalwart Carleton men showed. Yet above that came the answering cry from the loyal side—girls screeching like hysterical field mice with hawks close. He thought he heard one high-pitched shriek: "Loren! Loren!" but that was impossible.

The team went down to its section of the field and warmed up.

Coach Terwilliger called them together for a little talk. She said to get in there and break up plays, especially the Paso Verde reverse, and to fight clean and hard. Then she benched the reserves, nine or ten guys who shouldn't have been allowed near a football by their mothers.

"You're acting captain," she told Jacoby.

A couple of minutes later the game began, with Carleton winning the toss and electing to kick. Naturally, Dewar of Paso Verde scooped up the ball and ran for a touchdown—which Loren figured was about par for the evening, with a score a minute. They tried to pass for the extra point, but Hodges got lucky and batted it down.

Paso Verde put the ball into play with a bad kickoff which went out of bounds on the 40-yard line. On an off-tackle buck, Loren made four yards, which was unusual, and a pass from Jacoby to Martinez was good for a first down, which was even less likely.

It wasn't until the end of the first half that Carleton began to understand what was happening. They were holding Paso Verde from scoring, although twice in the second quarter they had to stand them off inside the 10.

A couple of guys in the line started to ask "how come," in the style of intimate conversation between guards. They got the answer. Paso Verde wasn't mopping up the earth with these Carleton rags and bones merely because half the northern team were sick with Asiatic fallout flu.

Furthermore, a tackle and a center intimated, playing against a team who had been coached by a woman English teacher was a frightening experience for honest, straightforward youths. Once they got the feel of the situation, the true murder would begin.

Still, the score at half time was 6 to 0, which was a Carleton victory in itself, even if they punched out ten or twelve touchdowns later. From then on, Carleton kids would say: "Remember when we had Paso Verde only one touchdown ahead at the half? Those were the days—back in the Terwilliger era."

There wasn't any half-time pep talk. Instead, Mr. Busch walked around among sprawled shapes and searched into each guy's health. He had a real interest in whether a person had acquired a busted leg or something. Evidently he thought that when somebody was injured or sick, he should lie down very quietly for a long time and let the trouble go away. A youth liked that kind of consideration.

When the call for the second half came, Alice Hodges came out with a peculiar idea. "To be, or not to be," he blatted, "that there is the question."

Bug Bugatti wanted to know what he meant.

"Dunno," Hodges told him, as puzzled as a mouse who happened to gnaw the live end of a match. "It just come out of nowhere. Well, let's get in and assassinate them jokers. Let's make their too, too solid flesh melt."

80

The whistle blew and the game resumed. Of course, Paso Verde began a power drive straight down midfield that ended with their second touchdown and a conversion. Stuff was back to normal.

By this time, everything had begun to buzz in Loren's mind—maybe because he'd been kicked in the head about four times. Also, Tuthouse kept giving him the ball for line plays, and the Paso Verde guys stopped him with shoe-top tackles that taught a person a fine lesson about the good earth. He did get away for a fair end run, and the stands squeaked into the chilly night as he tore along the sidelines. But he stepped out of bounds.

The Paso Verde drive sputtered out too, for some crazy reason. The third quarter ended without more scoring, and now the fourth was almost over.

Coach Terwilliger sent in Howard Johnson for Ritchie. Down in the huddle, he gave the message. "Old Lady—I mean Coach Terwilliger wants you to pass, you stupid dopes," he screamed so that the whole Paso Verde team heard him. "Start passing and keep it up."

"So all right," Jacoby hollered back. "I was going to do it until you had to tell everybody, Johnson." He was pretty mad.

Alice Hodges raised a conciliatory hand and reminded Teddy that Johnson talked like that everywhere—in class, on the field, at his dad's ranch where they ran a cow-calf operation.

"Cows like Howie a lot," Hodges insisted. "So why not you, Jacoby?"

Sure enough, the discussion got Carleton penalized for too much time in the huddle; so instead of passing, Jacoby made Tuthouse call for a buck over center and gave the ball to Loren.

Later on, everyone admitted that it could have been the coach's real strategy: send in Johnson and confuse

Paso Verde with his hollering. Whatever it was, they were caught off guard, and Loren made sixty yards. Herminio Garcia caught him on their 15 with a tackle people could hear in their own homes behind closed doors. He got up wondering why. Also what, and where.

Naturally, Jacoby threw two incompleted passes for a penalty, and Hodges was stopped cold at the line of scrimmage. Meanwhile, Loren wandered around in the backfield watching the interesting patterns of youths entangled. Nobody noticed him.

On fourth down, Jacoby took the hand-off and began to fade back for another pass. He fumbled, and Hodges recovered in a peculiar style, sort of with the ball at arms' length.

Although the whole field was whirling, Loren saw Alice down that way and got the message. They'd called for a place kick and he'd missed the signal. He dug in, took the short run, and booted her.

"Hey!" somebody yelled. "That was—"

"Sorry," Loren told Hodges, picking up a teammate. "Didn't know you—"

A second later, Alice was pounding him on the back. "It was good," he yelped. "A field goal. Man, you and I planned that one just right."

"Thanks," Loren told him. "It has been a lot of fun, and thank you, thank you for—"

He was drowned out by the Carleton band really giving with victory tumult—all eight pieces. The last time Carleton had scored on Paso Verde was four years ago, when Frank Tessler was here. Tessler, of course, had gone on to star at San Jose State, and everyone claimed it was his Carleton experience that made him the sort of triple-threat ace he'd turned out to be.

Officials were arguing, and finally they allowed the score.

82

"Hey, Wallace," Alice Hodges said in a scared voice. "You all right?"

"Fine," Loren said. "This after-game dance is the greatest, isn't it? That eight-piece combo over there sure knows the latest, and—"

He heard Hodges still talking, although from a distance. "Jacoby," Alice was saying, "you know how you always claim Wallace is gonna flip?"

"Yeah," Teddy answered. "Why?"

"Well, he's done it," Hodges came back. "Gonk! Like that."

Later, in the showers, he got oriented again—enough to know that the game ended 13–3. It was tough on Paso Verde to be humiliated in that style. A blot like only beating Carleton by ten points would be a heavy, heavy load on the record books for years to come.

In a way, Loren felt sorry for them all—good guys, a little heavy on the rough play, but clean in their sportsmanship.

CHAPTER 7 . . .

In the locker rooms after the Paso Verde game, Loren had remembered this was the night he was supposed to take Vada to the after-game dance. She'd even hinted as much today when he'd met her in the hall.

"Uh—Loren," she'd said, "I'm with the Girl Song Leaders, you know."

"I know," he'd answered, because who didn't? It was pretty hard for a group of women to jump around like that in front of everybody and not get recognized.

He recalled that she'd been devastatingly lovely and all that, with the kind of radiant energy girls had in the morning. But it was hard for him to pay attention. If he stayed here even one second longer, he'd realized, he could never make it to Mr. Busch's class, which was over in a temporary building put up during historic old World War II.

"Oh, you know?" she'd asked in a funny little voice.

"Yes." He'd dared to look straight at her; man, was she all right! He would have given anything to know her better, but naturally there wasn't a chance. "Why?"

That hadn't been a right question. She got mad, but of course girls were like that—sort of delicately balanced.

"Because I'll still be there, silly. In the stands when the game is over." Then she added, "Obviously."

He'd been able to grasp the gist. If she was waving arms with that great singing combo, she'd need to be in the stands. It was logical. "Sure," he'd told her.

Her eyes got narrower. "Well?" she'd asked. "Will I—will I meet you there, Loren, or—"

It wasn't likely, he'd decided, after giving the question plenty of thought. If he was down on the field following Terwilliger strategy, it would be difficult to run up into the stands and renew old friendships.

"Maybe—" he'd begun, meaning that he'd like to.

There had been a pause. Even Vada was probably beginning to realize they had to get to class.

She'd tapped her foot and sort of closed one eye. "Loren," she'd told him, "we are going to the after-game dance, aren't we? You will meet me in the stands after the game finishes, won't you?"

He'd gotten her message finally; she'd hinted that he could meet her near her song-leading girl buddies. It had taken that much time for him to penetrate the devious subtleties women liked to use to confuse men. With them it was only a game, probably.

"Oh—" he'd said. "Oh, sure, Vada. I'll—"

"How nice of you, Loren. To remember, I mean," Vada had said, and ducked into her class, which happened to be right there.

A little later, Mr. Hipper wasn't too convinced about his excuse for being late.

"You were just standing in the hall talking with a friend, and the time went by unnoticed, eh, Loren?" he'd asked.

"Yes."

The principal had examined records and stood at the counter, tapping bony fingers on the wood.

"You don't have many unexcused absences or tardiness," he'd said. "By the way, you're playing fullback tonight? Under the Terwilliger system?"

"Yes, sir," Loren had admitted.

Mr. Hipper had thought it over some more while he turned and stared out the window into a fading autumn. Loren couldn't help noticing how the sunshine glistened on his bald head.

At last, "I suppose that could make a boy absent-minded," the principal had said. "All right, I've given you an excused slip this time, but don't let it happen again."

"I won't," Loren had told him, meaning it. The chances of his ever going to another after-game dance with Vada Long were pretty remote. Most likely never.

Now in the locker rooms, his full awareness returned —right around subnormal. There was always the chance that Vada had really meant she would be waiting for him.

By the time he was dressed, the other guys had found out he wasn't one of those high school football casualties where the guy has permanent brain injury or drops dead. Hodges always claimed that could never happen in Carleton, because the victim needed a brain big enough to hurt.

Alice wanted to know why Loren had decided to kick a recovered fumble, but Jacoby took a different view.

"Meant to have Tuthouse call for a field goal all along," he said. "Wallace must have read my mind."

There was quite a bit of argument about the sort of skill needed to read a mind such as Jacoby's, but it was plain to Loren that the team liked putting up that kind of battle. At the dance, there wouldn't have to be the usual feeble jokes. A person could go in there and feel respectable.

Loren decided to get out of there, but Mr. Busch called him into the office.

"Feel all right?" he asked.

"Yes."

"You played a good game, Loren," the man said. "But I still think your real talents are in math and science."

"Thanks, Mr. Busch," Loren replied, glancing down.

The teacher was holding a big book he'd been reading, with a finger still stuck in the right place. The title was something about long-range weather prediction. Even in a tense game, he couldn't get his mind off science, maybe.

"Well, have a good time at the dance tonight," Mr. Busch said pleasantly. "Vada Long is certainly a fine girl."

"True," Loren told him, and went outside.

He was halfway across the field toward the bleachers before it hit him that his math mentor had plenty of information about his private life. But who was he to reason why? Teachers seemed to possess a lot more savvy than most people gave them credit for having.

By then he'd spotted a clump of girls still screeching around near the midfield. He recognized Shirlee Danforth right away because she was so tall, but he saw Vada too.

Of course, there was always the chance she'd changed her mind and would give him one of those haughty stares that pierce right through a person. It was too late to turn back; he plowed on.

Shirlee saw him. She had a tall voice too, and she used it. "Loren," she cried out, "we heard you get kicked in the head and it sounded just like a melon, didn't it, kids? It went 'thump' in a sick style you could hear all over the field."

It had, at that. Now that he remembered, his head sounded like a bad watermelon—only worse when you heard it from the inside.

But no use admitting you were a melon-head, at least not in public. "I—" he began, meaning to say it was maybe more like a gourd, "I don't think—"

Right there, Vada Long ran over and sort of surrounded him so he felt as if he was in the center of a troop of Girl Scouts. "Are you sure you're all right, Loren?" she implored. "Perhaps we'd better not go to the dance, if—"

"Fine—" he grunted, meaning that he was in as good shape for a dance this way as he would be healthy.

She looked him over like an exhibit at the fair. "Maybe," Vada said doubtfully. "Well, we can go there, but—"

She had begun to steer him away across the field.

"By," she waved to her buddies. "See you."

He heard his feet scuffling along in the grass, and if he could do that he could dance about as well as usual. At last they'd made it over to the gym, with Vada talking and Loren holding up his end of the conversation by saying, "Yeah," and, "That's right," every so often. They liked a person to contribute to their mad notions.

He could hear the golden brass of the horns lip out the note, with the electric guitars backing up the rhythm with plenty of that hysterical, rich, nerve-busting twang that a teen-ager realized was genuine music. Just before they went inside, he saw that there was a full moon tonight hung on the line of sky, with torn black clouds ripping across it from high-altitude winds. And with that perfect woman beside him, this was real living!

Long afterward, when he realized that he actually enjoyed that dance, he understood the secret so often described in poem and book. All a guy needed to get the true ecstasy was to let himself be kicked in the head beforehand. With his tender young brains jarred out of place that way, he could pitch himself into the spirit.

Even so, he noticed that Carleton after-game dances were fairly drab. There were no decorations in the gym, and the orchestra was a local combo featuring a youth whose parents had given him an electric guitar by mistake one Christmas. Neighbors made up a petition so he couldn't even practice in city limits. But in him music found a way, sort of in the manner Mozart persisted. He'd wired up an abandoned railroad water tower and amplified his art under those conditions. Talent? The guy really had it.

Loren and Vada had the first dance together, but he didn't say anything because he was too busy steering through the mob. Once, though, they reached a quiet corner spot where the electric guitar didn't throb quite so much tempo in a youth's very own head. He risked glancing down at her. She was looking right back, with her eyes and lips muted by the soft light.

"Are you—?" he began, meaning to ask her if she was standing the pace all right. A person was supposed to look out for the comfort of a woman he was escorting. His mother even said so.

"Yes," she told him. "I am."

She never did get to tell him what she was, because Alice Hodges and Shirlee came charging down toward them, so Loren had to swerve. No use getting trampled.

It was one of those tender moments of high school, he guessed, that a guy kept storing up in his unconscious mind and remembered about a hundred years later when he looked at the annual.

The number ended. He jigged around with other women—some here, some there, until finally toward the last he danced a few more times with Vada, and the enchanting evening got done so people could go home and hit the sack.

There was a lot of stalling around while women yelped their fond farewells, before he could get the girl into his car to take her home. After a few maneuvers to get out of the parking lot with a couple of fenders left, they reached the open road.

Before long, they crossed the bridge over the Salinas, killed a right up the river road, and reached her home, where someone had left the gate open. He saw cattle shadows in an adjacent fenced field which was an island of moonlight, and he thought of Walter. That calf would probably have enjoyed the dance tonight as much as he did.

Here was her house at the crescent of the driveway, now dark as sleep. He cut the lights and eased to a stop with the engine silent. No use to alarm her father needlessly. He put out a hand to the latch to get out and open the door for her. Merely courtesy. She probably was as beat as he, and delicate women needed shut-eye as much as humans, probably.

"What do you think of Mr. Busch, Loren?" she asked, sort of leaning back as if she'd decided to rest right there.

It was a leading question. "Well—" he began. Mr. Busch was the sort of educator a youth didn't need to think about on his own time.

"He's nice," Vada said, "but—"

Loren nodded. It about summed up the science teacher, at that.

There was a silence. Then: "I heard him trying to get the Almond Grove game postponed from Friday night to Saturday afternoon. It was something about the arc lights and giving Coach Blount an extra day to get well. Don't you think that would interfere with the Football Frolic? It's traditional to have it after the Almond Grove game, but if the game is Saturday afternoon, it wouldn't leave us much time to get ready for the dance, would it?"

She had a funny tone in her voice, probably from worrying about Coach Blount's health.

"I don't know," he replied. "What did Mr. Hipper say?"

Vada sounded surprised. "You mean—about the Football Frolic?"

"No. About the postponement."

She laughed like these tin bells. "He told Mr. Busch to go ahead, and that no effort, however small, to relieve Miss Terwilliger would be wasted."

It figured. No use in wearing down a fine old English teacher.

"I—" he started to say, "agr—"

90

He happened to notice that talking over mundane stuff of Carleton life had got him a lot closer to Vada. She was right there, man.

Jacoby had hit truth; around here people were flipping every day, and he was one of them.

"Vada—" he said, kind of desperately.

"Yes, Loren—"

It was the soft, throaty way of innocent women that got him, he guessed. He gulped and plunged on, heedless that he was taking advantage even though she went steady with Morgan.

"Would you—?"

She waited. "Yes, would I—?"

"Go with me— to—?"

Diabolically clever as he'd been, he hadn't planned ahead. When a girl went with a youth somewhere, she probably wanted a definite idea of what he had in mind. Frantically, he tried to think of a place she might want to go. Salinas, or— Out, maybe.

Vada made a muffled sound, like a giggle held back with woman-force. "Yes, Loren," she said. "I'd love to go with you to—"

It was his lucky night. From nowhere, the name of a school function hit him. "The Football Frolic," he managed.

She was terribly serious. "I'd love to go with you to the Football Frolic," she told him, "and thank you, thank you ever so—"

He noticed that she'd stopped and was looking at him in an accusing style. He knew why. Right when she was yakking, a mad compulsion to kiss her had grabbed him, and it must have shown on his face.

Vada didn't say a word for a long time—maybe thirty seconds. Instead, she merely observed him reproachfully, with her eyes half closed and the corners of her mouth turned up a little, like a smile that wasn't a smile at all. Only woman's way.

Sure, he'd almost made an idiot of himself thinking he could kiss Bobby Morgan's girl. But he got by that. "I'd better take you in," he said.

He did. He got out and opened the car door for her, walking in abject silence to her front door.

"Good night, Loren," she said. "I've had a lovely evening."

Then she went inside.

He got out of there, but not right away. When he tried to start his car, he flooded it and spent some time grinding the mill. But the engine finally caught, and a good thing, too.

CHAPTER 8 . . .

CARLETON HIGH SCHOOL was slow to recover from the strain of coming so close to beating Paso Verde. Football fever was in the air, infectious and all, as they said, and it might have risen by degrees if there had been a game to play. But Redwood Haven, a private school over in the valley and next on the schedule, canceled because Asiatic fallout flu had decimated their team. They were nonleague and didn't make any difference in the standings, but a default naturally caused a letdown in school spirit.

It was typical Carleton luck, people said. The team, fired up by Coach Terwilliger's gridiron wizardry, probably could have won, even though a private school was so much better than public schools academically. They said so themselves. There was an equalizing factor with Redwood Haven. It had a student body about the same size as Carleton's.

One rumor around school was that Mr. Hipper was responsible for the cancellation because he claimed that none of the buses would make it that far. According to informed sources, the principal had tried to keep the board from scheduling any games over ten miles from home.

"You gentlemen don't have to drive those antiquated

piles of cast iron," he was reported to have said. "There's a fifteen percent grade into the Sierras to get to Redwood Haven. Our buses quit at five percent. Make them come over here if you like. It's downhill all the way."

Some of the guys who had to ride the buses agreed with Mr. Hipper. Jo-Jo Maller said that a trip to Redwood Haven would mean pushing the bus at least a hundred miles by hand, and even fired-up youths didn't have that kind of strength. Others with their own transportation hinted that it was a clear case of the principal not having the courage to stand firm. A game with Redwood Haven, they insisted, was exactly what the team needed to whet killer instinct for Almond Grove the following week. Also it would improve Carleton's success image around town.

Another fantastic rumor floating here and there was that the Almond Grove game was going to be postponed from Friday night to Saturday afternoon. It had something to do with Carleton's arc lights being shorted and only putting out half power, but that was impossible. Local arcs were only about half efficient anyway.

As for Loren, he didn't know what to believe. That way he was a lot like Hamlet. The ghost had finally admitted that he was his father who had been murdered by his uncle—which didn't indicate too good a family relationship.

It was fairly hard to believe ghosts too much, even back then, so Hamlet had gone around pretending to be crazy until people believed he was. By reenacting the murder in a play, he'd become convinced that his uncle, the new king, was acting awfully guilty.

While he was talking to his mother about the murder, he thought he smelled a rat and whipped out his sword to stab through a nearby screen. Polonius happened to be hiding there and got killed, so the king didn't feel too comfortable having Hamlet in the house, crazy and all.

94

He arranged to have a couple of henchmen take his nephew to England and have a bad accident. Through the whole deal, Hamlet still had trouble making up his mind.

Because of the nutty way he acted, Ophelia got mixed up, and also it was hard for her to understand why Hamlet stabbed her father. Finally she got pretty maladjusted and couldn't conform to her environment, so she fell into the creek and drowned. That didn't help out much in their love.

With Loren it was the opposite; he was mixed up, partly from being kicked in the head and partly from the way Vada Long had acted.

Vada had been right. Mr. Busch had indeed wanted the game with Almond Grove postponed from Friday night until Saturday afternoon. But it was not precisely for the reasons set forth.

True, the Carleton arc lights were unsuited to night games, and the additional day might return Coach Blount to the field. Yet, as Mr. Busch had to admit himself, later events proved it was as much to test his volcano theory as for any other purpose.

Oh, certainly, he had a genuine regard for Carleton youth and wanted to do something that would boost their morale. But, for that matter, he actually liked Miss Terwilliger too. He saw in that massive teacher a declining breed, similar to the carrier pigeon or the whooping crane. Yet, for pinhead accuracy, she was better compared with a stopped clock which is right at least twice a day. In her educational methods, she had been correct years and years ago; now momentarily she was right again. He had that affection for the past which treasures a rare antique around the place.

Miss Terwilliger, on the other hand, had been almost totally wrong in her appraisal of Mr. Busch. He was frail, to be sure; his muscles, strong as rubber bands, were nevertheless adequate to propel him from place to place and do the work according to the need. But beyond that he did not tax them. Whenever pointless work or athletic endeavors came his way, he felt an overpowering weakness compel him to sit down somewhere and reason why.

However, he was far from sniggly, nor was he brash. Instead, he had a friendly, outgoing personality which sought after peaceful forbearance and calm relationships. In this he was joined by his pretty, frail young wife and his three young children.

They all liked Carleton and hated to leave. From signs and portents, such as his salary check and a few other clues any teacher who believed in the "whole child" concept could easily read, he knew he had to move on next year. If anyone pulled a few backstage wires to help Carleton High School, he was the logical choice.

Also, it was one of those contradictions that Hugh Busch, as mild and harmless as a man can get and still be alive, was fascinated by active volcanoes and studied them the way other scholars paw through books. On his honeymoon with Adela years ago, back when they had enough money to take a honeymoon, he had seen mighty Kilauea in eruption. Later, by scrimping and saving, he'd managed to visit another only a few miles out of Guatemala City.

He admired their innate truth. One could be capped for a time, betraying only a slight restlessness, thus lulling local inhabitants. Then, on a calm night, the explosion, the deluge of fiery ashes and molten rock. They were beautiful and pure.

Aside from this aesthetic regard for the awesome, unpredictable power of a volcano, Mr. Busch had independently evolved a theory which to his satisfaction was now propounded by at least one important scientist. It was that, the natural purpose of volcanoes was as earthly thermostats on a grand planetary scale.

The quantity and distribution of volcanic matter in the air, he firmly believed, had a profound effect upon what happened here below. And he had reasons. Time after time, his amateur predictions had proved absolutely correct almost to the hour, especially when used with conventional long-range data.

It could be that he had acquired his mild character as much through association with volcanoes as from his puny size. The power of those natural works had made any strong man or group of strong men seem insignificant to Hugh Busch. It was therefore his dream to get a teaching job near an active volcano, although he doubted such good luck could ever happen to him. Consequently, he had applied early to the superintendent at Hilo, Hawaii, practically at Kilauea's doorstep. To his amazement, he had received a tentative reply. Now all he could do was hope.

Mr. Busch was a fine teacher of science and math who genuinely liked his students both objectively and in the abstract.

Loren Wallace, for example, demanded abstraction. He reminded the teacher so much of himself when a youth that the similarity was laughable. Also sad. Not physically, of course; the Wallace kid was easily six feet tall and still growing, to judge by his appearance of imminent collapse —like some leaning tower of pizza.

Rather, it was the haunting, hunted look of inner torment and self-doubt that was all too familiar, as if sleuths of adolescence were closing in upon the unbearably guilty. Mr. Busch knew what it meant to be that young, having only recently outgrown the condition, as accelerated men frequently do at age thirty-five or so.

Objectively, naturally, he also liked pretty Vada Long, one of those girl students who delight the educator's jaundiced eye and ease his weary mind. She reminded Mr. Busch of Adela when they had first met as high school sophomores. Young, bright, terribly cool and intense and wonderfully loyal—the kind of girl who could even marry a schoolteacher and last the full distance, if fate were that unkind.

By natural insight, he realized that Vada liked Loren, as did quite a few other Carleton girls—although that youth seemed totally unaware of his dumbheaded charm. The girl, herself, had clinched that speculation into fact.

She had come in to see Mr. Busch one afternoon when classes were over. It was to find out something "tangible" of what went on in the science department for the school paper, which bore the stamp of Terwilliger advice.

He was giving out the usual: that science teaching at Carleton was the solid, tough-subject, inexpensive, ever-expanding, modern, and patriotic space-age study designed to meet today's challenges with tomorrow's tax dollar. At that point, Loren came blundering in.

"Something?" Mr. Busch had inquired.

The youth had looked exactly like a startled young Olympia elk who had blustered into an armed camp, believing it to be the sheltering pines. With terrified elk-eyes on Vada, he had backed away toward the door.

"Owk—ulp," he had said pleasantly. "Didn't know. Come back later." Then he had fled, taking his velvety antlers with him.

After a decent interval, Mr. Busch had asked, "What's wrong with him?"

"I— I don't know," Vada had said impetuously. "But I surely wish I did. Do you, Mr. Busch? Do you know what's wrong with him?"

A science teacher was able to make scientific deductions, of course. "He seems awfully bashful. I'd say he likes you, Vada."

He'd glanced at her and witnessed a sight seldom seen these days in class and hallway. The girl's face had actually flushed with color, and though impossible, it had improved upon perfection. Her brown eyes were veiled with shadowy lashes; her hair asked sincere, scientific questions of the gold in the afternoon sunshine; her nose uptilted, while all innocence ringed about her in a shining shield.

"I'm— I'm sure he doesn't," she'd said. "He's— he's kind of strange in a funny way. Nice, I mean, but—"

She'd left immediately afterward, with the Carleton science education picture only half exposed. But half was probably quite enough.

Later, by observation and evaluation, he had reached a definite conclusion. Vada and Loren liked each other but had not yet made necessary arrangements for that charming discovery.

Shy boys like Loren had troubles, sure, but girls endured a few problems all their own. It wasn't easy for a girl to get a nice, stupid boy to understand her—especially if that girl was brighter in a nicer way.

What the lad needed was a little self-confidence, of course, so when the occasion arose, he could say, "I like you, Vada." And everything would be easier. The trouble was that young Wallace had so little to be self-confident about. Excellent grades in math and science weren't enough, Mr. Busch knew from personal experience, and had not helped him with gaining necessary verve back in the old days. But placing first in the class C hundred-yard dash at a dual meet against what surely must have been handicapped children had done wonders. As he recalled it, a discussion begun by Adela about his magnificent prowess in the dash to glory had emboldened him to ask her for a date.

Yet there seemed small chance for athletic heroism in Loren. Like so many others on the Carleton team, the youth was a positive hindrance to forward motion, unless—And there, Mr. Busch had hit upon his cunning scheme.

In a sense, it was for Loren Wallace that the science teacher sought a postponement of the Almond Grove game. Naturally, it was a long chance and not in the proper spirit of high school sportsmanship. Yet the evening of odds had always been an American standard. The great equalizer in the winning of the West had been the Colt revolver. Now, in the struggle between powerful Almond Grove and puny Carleton, it could well be Hugh Busch.

He had thought through most of the details. While he knew nothing of the gridiron, he was very familiar with the principles of viscosity and objects in motion. His double-thumb-lock technique for grasping and hurling a football under anticipated conditions was satisfactory, and a few soil tests had perfected the system. The soil around the Carleton field had exactly enough clay content to produce spectacular results.

Thus prepared, he had gone to Mr. Hipper, having called Coach Blount's doctor and knowing the faulty condition of Carleton's arc lights.

Long ago, Mr. Busch had taken the principal's measure. The man was overworked and underpaid. He had lost control of his school board long ago, and an attitude of resignation was upon him.

The board wanted a return to "basic education," an eleven-man football team, improved teaching methods, greater attention to math and science, new ideas, teaching machines, elimination of problem students, indoctrination for superpatriotism, plenty of democracy, and freedom.

Yet it was opposed to paying even one extra dime for doing the job. The decrepit old buildings, the board thought, had served the youth in the past, and they saw no reason why they weren't still good enough, even though state condemnation was inevitable. Now, with consolidation and a new bond issue on the same ballot at the special election next week, both Mr. Hipper and Mr. Busch could foretell the result. Carleton citizens, good men and true, would vote down consolidation while at the same time defeating the bonds.

The analysis proved correct.

"An extra day?" Mr. Hipper had sighed, looking over his glasses in a harassed style, rather like a bewildered jackrabbit only one jump ahead of the coyotes, Mr. Busch thought. "Why?"

The science teacher had explained.

"I know about the arcs. Can't be helped. But you say Blount might be back. Are you sure, Busch?"

"Dr. Warner said that nobody could be certain with Asiatic pneumonia. But it's possible. The coach is home now and recuperating normally."

Mr. Hipper had become almost pathetically thoughtful. "Yes, I see. It would mean that Miss Terwilliger wouldn't be—"

He'd stopped momentarily. Then, in a burst of confidence, the principal told facts—that the idea of a woman football coach was likely to gain wider publicity.

"I've had calls from as far away as San Francisco," he'd said. "Big city feature editors want the details, Busch. They might all be down here for the game. Imagine the story—headlines—photo coverage—"

Mr. Busch had to nod. It was entirely possible. The odd, the bizarre, the exotic, and the plain stupid all had strong appeal to newspaper readers.

"Amazon English teacher coaches team of all-American boys in Carleton," he'd whispered, suggesting a headline. "It could be picked up by press associations and published in—"

"A thousand papers," the principal finished. "Wherever we went from that moment on, Busch—" he'd quavered, "they'd remember. You know how school boards can recall the record."

"I do," Hugh Busch had agreed, noticing that Mr. Hipper had already picked up the phone.

As it turned out, Almond Grove was willing to be generous. It didn't make any difference to them how Carleton wanted to take the customary bloodshed—standing up, lying down, on Friday or Saturday. Thus, by obtaining a day's delay, Coach Blount might be back on the field, reporters thwarted, and the memories of school boards kept unsullied.

"Uh—" said Mr. Hipper, "Busch, perhaps you'd better explain to Old Lad—to our Miss Terwilliger. After all, you're the assistant coach, and—"

"Right, Chief," Busch had said. "I'll tell her." Which proved that a man's size had nothing to do with his enormous courage. "I'm sure Miss Terwilliger will understand."

"Oh, naturally," Mr. Hipper had said as his dauntless science teacher left the office. "And—and good luck, Busch, old man."

Briefly, Miss Terwilliger's assistant had considered taking that lady into full confidence, starting with the volcano theory and going on from there. Yet human volcanoes were seldom interested in natural ones. Besides, he knew instinctively that her rockbound integrity would never allow the slightest adjustment for inequalities of strength. Her philosophy of the game was doubtless simple and straightforward—kill or be killed. If Carleton youths were going to get clobbered, let them get in there and take it like men.

He had finally decided upon bare facts. On Monday afternoon he went directly to the field instead of to the gym. From a distance, Mr. Busch thought she must be wearing a nose guard, but it was only her regular face.

102

As he approached Miss Terwilliger, he realized again why the team was so quiet in the locker rooms. Grim fear, he supposed, had made them old before their time.

"Yes," said the English teacher when he was within range. "What is it now, Mr. Busch?"

He had to admit there was something majestic about Lanetta Terwilliger, almost like old Britannia still ruling the waves. She had that militant air in her divided skirt, black blouse, baseball cap, tennis shoes, and whistle. Also she was wearing sunglasses, which hid her steely eyes.

He'd called her by first name a time or two, but that didn't seem appropriate now. "Coach," he said, noticing that his normally baritone voice had slipped up the scale a notch or two.

There weren't going to be any cordial step-by-step explanations between colleagues, he could tell.

"Mr. Busch," she snapped testily, "I've been told by the office that this Almond Grove postponement was your idea. Is that so?"

She had folded her arms like Chief Crazy Horse who didn't plan any peace pipe nonsense this time around. Just plenty of scalping.

"Well—" he began, "I thought—"

"Indeed?" she said, surprised. "How very novel."

For an instant, Mr. Busch speculated upon what a course in junior English from the coach would be like. Why, after a year with Lanetta a youth might wake up at night with conjunctive adverbs and elliptical clauses burned indelibly into his sensitive subconscious. Years later, he could manifest a nervous twitch whenever he encountered a sentence like "However hard he tries, he will fail," or "While on duty, my foot slipped."

"I—" he began, trying to get started on a calm outline of the facts.

"Speak up," said the coach. "You—"

A peculiar thing happened to Mr. Busch. Suddenly, in this awesome pedagogical presence, he began to feel like Dr. Jekyll when Hyde took over. A creepy, sneaky weakness engulfed him, and there he was again—little Hughie Busch, about fifteen years old.

"I just had a hunch, Coach," he blurted.

Miss Terwilliger's lips compressed to an even grimmer line, but then the corners of her mouth uprose about a thirty-second of an inch. She was smiling, he realized with an imperceptible shudder. Somehow, he had brought out Lanetta's gentler nature.

"So you just had a hunch," she said severely. "I suppose you realize that hunches are not a suitable excuse for postponing an—an engagement?"

"Yes, Coach," he said faintly. "I do."

There was a silence, weighted with justice like a guillotine.

"The harm's done," she said. "There's nothing we can do about it now, is there, Hugh?"

"Unh-unh," he answered, feeling even younger—about ten. If he didn't get out of here fast, she'd be mixing him up a formula. His eyes strayed toward the gym and freedom. "I—I guess I'd better go now."

"Yes," Coach Terwilliger told him crisply. "The boys are all in there by now, Hugh. You'd better run along like a good—"

He didn't hear the last word because he'd got going. Not running, mind you, or even trotting. But hastening.

Back on the field, the coach watched him for a moment, fingering the silvery whistle that hung around her neck. She was annoyed, but the postponement would give her team an extra afternoon of practice.

Behind her dark glasses, there was a strange glint of victory in battle. Her opinion of Mr. Busch hadn't changed —not a whit or an iota; he was still as sniggly as ever.

104

Yet she felt kindlier toward him. As in all brash men, there was plenty of awkward boy remaining. In a way, she regretted that poor little Hugh hadn't been here in Carleton to take English from her. All he needed was basic education, strong discipline, a few sessions with conjunctive adverbs, and all that sniggliness might have been corrected. She'd done the job on any number of similar boys in her time.

Nothing could be done now; it was too late. She lifted her eyes and saw the team coming out of the gym, on the double.

It was good, but it could be better. She raised the whistle and blew a wintry blast and smiled once more, the way she had done to put Hugh Busch at his ease. Those ahead had begun to run vigorously, like young Newfoundland puppies who knew their master when they saw her.

CHAPTER 9 . . .

IT WAS SATURDAY, with the Almond Grove game only a week away. Night had set in, and the locker rooms at Carleton High should have been at rest, but they weren't. Four youths were there, ready to go home at last —Loren Wallace and three buddies, Hodges, Jacoby, and Tuthouse, the backfield, such as it was.

Jacoby gestured toward the office where Mr. Busch sat. "What'd I tell you, Wallace?" he whispered, making a popping sound with his tongue as of someone pulling the cork on the brain bottle.

Reluctantly, Loren had to nod; there wasn't any other explanation. Now Mr. Busch was motioning to them, so all four walked that way together for protection. Once inside the door, all waited silently.

"You did fine," said Mr. Busch. "Loren, you caught on to the double-thumb clutch splendidly, and, Teddy, you were especially alert at receiving. Hodges and Tuthouse did fine too."

Nobody answered, because there was nothing to say.

Mr. Busch smiled. "Remember, not a word of this to anyone. This was secret practice, and fortunately nobody saw us out there behind the Ag building. Can you all come back tomorrow afternoon?"

Silence.

Loren began to feel embarrassed for Mr. Busch. Even though he was nutty about football, he was sound as a bell in everything else. It was best to humor a teacher.

"I'll be there, Coach," he said.

"Good," Mr. Busch came back. "How about the rest of you?"

There was another long pause.

Finally Alice Hodges cleared his throat. "Mr. Busch," he asked, "can I say a question?"

"Certainly," replied the science teacher, leaning back in the swivel chair and making a sort of cage with his fingertips pressed together. "Fire away."

While Loren and the others stared at him helpfully, Alice tried to phrase it just right. His bushy brows drew down and gave him about an inch of forehead. Concentration.

"What are we doing?" Hodges asked. "I mean, I don't get it noway. It don't make much—I mean, I do not understand what is going on, Mr. Busch."

The teacher permitted the swivel chair to bounce him forward, and Loren noticed the guys stepping back involuntarily. "Boys," he said, "you promised you wouldn't talk about this with anyone."

"I won't," Hodges admitted. "I don't plan to tell nobody about this, ever."

"Me, either," Tuthouse and Jacoby said, almost together.

Mr. Busch's eyes grew dreamy and faraway. "Volcanoes," began the science teacher, "are very important to—" He stopped. "But I suppose that would be too complicated and drawn out. Later on I'll explain it. Right now you boys want to get home. Let's put it this way for brevity," the teacher continued. "It might happen to rain."

"Rain?" somebody asked hoarsely.

"Yes. While you're playing Almond Grove, rain could fall. So—"

"Oh, sure," said Alice Hodges, getting the picture. "So you've had us practicing them slippery-elm passes because—"

"Exactly," came back Mr. Busch in an admiring tone for a bright pupil. "If it—happened to rain, you'd be—er, prepared. Loren has already learned to pass accurately under those conditions, and the rest of you are showing the ability to hang on to that kind of ball."

Jacoby put on his best teacher-talk style. "Oh, I get it," he came in soothingly. "Be prepared in the same manner we used to do in Boy Scouts. I understand, Mr. Busch."

"I'd hoped you would," the man said. "Now we'd all better get home. We'll meet here tomorrow afternoon at two and run through the drill again. Later in the week, we'll have more practice sessions if I can arrange them."

"Right, Coach," Loren offered uncertainly.

As if on signal, the four began to sidle out of the office, moving sort of backward so they could see what Mr. Busch was going to do next.

Suddenly, the little teacher laughed. "Don't worry so much," he told them pleasantly. "Please just trust me, boys. I think I know what I'm doing."

Outside, Jacoby was first to speak. "Hear the laugh?" he asked, shivering. "Ghoulish, wasn't it? And he thinks it might rain. Guys, Busch is gone. Brain waves from the hospital, I expect. They reached out and grabbed him—"

"Wait a second," Loren had to say. "It really could rain." He liked Mr. Busch, and no telling what the new science teacher would be after they hauled him away. "Every so often it rains around here. Also, the weather is different."

Tuthouse shook his head. "There you go, Wallace, sticking up for the system. Me, I don't know. I think—"

"It ain't right practice for playing a game in the rain even if it did sprinkle," Alice butted in. "Whoever heard of passing a football dipped in that there mud of his, or—"

108

"Yeah," Tuthouse added. "And how about his spraying us with the Ag building fire hose? Wallace, you ever see rain around here like that?"

"No, but—"

At that, it had been fairly unusual. First, Mr. Busch had made them report in old jeans and T-shirts. Then he'd dipped the ball in a bucket of thin mud and acted like a fireman stopping a riot. It could cause questions around town about basic education.

At that, the science teacher sure knew his mud. He'd shown Loren a way to lock his thumb on one side of the ball and press down the whole flat of his hand on the other. It gave more traction, and after a while he'd become pretty accurate in his tosses. Mr. Busch had taught Jacoby and the others to let the whole soggy mess get cradled by arms against a chest or a stomach. It worked. They'd concentrated on short throws, but even a couple of long ones were good.

Another thing: Busch's mud wasn't like the ordinary variety. It was as slippery as grease, and something around the consistency of pancake batter mixed with syrup. Without the double-thumb-lock technique, no human could hang on to the ball.

"And another thing," Jacoby said. "Notice that bunch of maps on his desk?"

"Maps? What do them things have to do with mud?"

"That's it," Teddy confided. "Nothing. Still, he's playing with maps. One was a forestry issue. You know—topographical, and of this county. The other one was bigger, and it's of the Pacific Ocean. Guys, it was marked with red circles, arrows, and stuff. He's planning this mud kick on a global scale."

They had reached the parking lot. For a while, the buddies leaned on hood and fenders while Loren got around inside to start the engine.

"Men," Teddy continued, "it's a scary world for us unspoiled youths to grow up in. How about Coach Terwilliger's 'To be, or not to be' secret play? You know, where everybody in the whole backfield handles the ball at least once before we even try to take it somewhere?"

The car started, and Loren let it idle, warming up. His true friends piled in.

"Yeah, ain't it the truth?" Alice Hodges moaned, sprawling out in the back seat. "But what can us youths do about it? Nothing. So we do what Ol' Lady Terwilliger says at regular practice, we get out on our own time for Busch's mud call, and next week the voters are going to vote down bonds and consolidation. My dad even says so. We're nothin' but prawns in their fishy game, see?"

Everyone saw.

Since it was Saturday and not yet suppertime, all three buddies wanted to be let out downtown—which in this case was the drugstore.

"Going to be there tomorrow?" Loren asked.

"Sure," Jacoby said in a defeated style. "We promised, didn't we? No use to buck a trend."

That was probably true, Loren realized. There wasn't a chance that the science teacher was right. The rainy season around here began in January, at the same time ranchers started to complain about bad conditions in nature and the Government.

"Suppose Coach Blount did come back?" he ventured. "Then—"

"Wouldn't do a bit of good. Not now," Alice Hodges said, dropping his hands and arms so they hung there around his knees. He liked to let people know that it was earlier than they thought, and the ape in a guy was still mighty real. "We were a fine little team when he took sick because of Tuthouse towels. Now look at us: coached by a woman, with the assistant coach making us play mud

110

pies. Know what we'll be called all over the league?"

Nobody did.

"The mud hens," Hodges sneered. "Baby mud hens."

Loren took off, and later that evening Jacoby telephoned.

"There's a great bill at the drive-in," he claimed. "It's that one where a person isn't supposed to reveal the plot. You know, about that American diplomat who gets sick. In the hospital they brainwash and rewire him. He has to follow orders from this Mongolian queen and stuff. Everyone says it's a blast. Real psychology."

At that, the movie wasn't bad. All the ads insisted that it would hold people in such terrifying suspense that they would have to scream the whole time, and to please never reveal the shocking climax. The film was a good change of pace from monsters.

Nevertheless, Loren's attention strayed a few times when he got to remembering the after-game dance he'd gone to with Vada. Somehow or other he'd asked her to go to the Football Frolic, but now he wasn't sure.

He'd met her in the hall a few times, and she'd talk, all right, but she never mentioned their date. Also she'd say something like, "Loren Wallace, are you listening to me?"

They asked questions like that. Maybe his ears were supposed to waggle as a sign. He'd be hearing every word—regular sweet nothings—and trying to think of what to say back.

"Why?" he'd mentioned.

"Because you don't act as if you're listening. I said, how is the team getting along? You know, for the game right before the Football Frolic?"

"So-so," he'd told her.

She'd waited awhile. Then, "Is—is that all you're going to say?"

"Muddy in the backfield," he'd added.

More waiting.

"I thought so," she'd told him. "Well, good-by now, Loren."

She'd gone away.

It meant that his love wasn't doing so fine, because she hadn't given him a hint this time. Love was pretty gossamer if they expected a guy to listen to them in a certain way and waggle his ears. Vada Long was pure enigma.

Once his dad had tried to tell him about women, and it all boiled down to Dr. Wallace's maintaining that the real secret about them was how girls liked boys about as well as boys liked girls. But naturally he was talking about women who lived in olden times, back when he was a youth. Everyone knew they'd changed a lot since then and become complicated.

Right now, Jacoby poked him. "Wallace," the guy said, pointing, "see that bomb over there? No, not that one. In the next lane. The hardtop with the chrome wheels."

Loren stared. "I see it. Neat."

Teddy chuckled. "That," he advised, "is the understatement of the instant. But I'm not discussing the car. Belongs to Bobby Morgan, naturally."

Loren took another long view. Drive-in theaters had plenty of darkness and romantic solitude. But sure enough, he could make out Morgan, all right, mostly from his haircut and the way his skull sat on a powerful neck.

The speaker in the car gave off a couple of good screams, but they came from the story sound track and not from witnesses.

"I see him," he said.

"Don't mean Morgan, Loren. Take a good look at the women in there with him."

He did. A couple of girls sat in the front seat with

112

Almond Grove's star. He didn't know either one. A guy wasn't that familiar with their individual mad hairstyle.

"The one in the middle looks a lot like Vada Long," Jacoby chuckled. "Gets around, that girl does."

Loren's heart sank like a lead baboon. The middle one did look like Vada. She had turned to hear something cute and wise from that idiot, Morgan, and it had to be her. She was giggling in her cute, infuriating style while Bobby had his curly head back, laughing hard at his own wonderful technique with the women.

He shut his eyes and turned away from the sight.

"So what?" he demanded stiffly. "She wants to be here in the drive-in, she can."

"All right, all right," Jacoby came back defensively. "Who said she couldn't? Just thought you'd like to know where your girl was, is all."

"My girl? Who said she was my girl?"

Jacoby sounded disbelieving. "You don't know? I mean, you haven't heard who says so?"

"No."

Teddy shrugged. "Then I'm not going to tell you, Wallace. You don't catch me butting in. It's not healthy psychology."

It was probably true. "Thanks," Loren said.

The movie ended with the American diplomat back to normal. True love had plenty to do with his recovery, as usual.

In the line of cars pulling out of there, the one behind honked a few times.

"It's Morgan," Jacoby said, turning around. "Why can't he get off that horn? He can tell we aren't able to get out of here any faster."

Loren didn't even look.

"Now he's got the girls shaking their fists at us or something," Teddy said. "How do you like that?"

"Let them do it," Loren said listlessly. "It's a free country."

"The one with Vada is a good-sized red-haired type," Jacoby added. "Kind of like Miss Terwilliger, only a lot younger."

They made the open road, killed a left, and got away from there.

After that, time dragged on and it was Sunday, at two. The four mud hens were back at the gym to find Mr. Busch waiting for them. Today he was dressed in old pants and a worn shirt.

"Fine!" the teacher told them when they were dressed. "Before we begin, I think I should explain much further to you boys. You see, volcanoes have an enormous effect on the upper atmosphere. There have been some splendid eruptions in the last few months—in Guatemala and the Pacific regions. By this time the powdery ash is well distributed above the various normal cold fronts. The effect is to absorb the solar heat over vast regions, and—"

He glanced around. "Are you following me?"

"No," said Alice Hodges, "I ain't followed none of it."

Mr. Busch sighed. "I suppose not," wistfully. "As I said before, you'll simply have to trust me."

A couple of minutes later they were behind the Ag building again, running through mud practice. Today, however, the teacher laid off the fire hose. It was perhaps a good thing. Yesterday's water had left a deep mudhole.

"No need for more," the teacher yelled happily, dipping the football. "Now I'll center. Tuthouse, you give the hand-off to Loren, and he'll pass to Teddy and Alice."

They ran through the play a few times. Surprisingly, Loren completed every throw he tried.

"Wonderful," Mr. Busch said, standing up. He had a red swath of Carleton mud across his face, and his hands were deep in it to the elbows. "Let's rest awhile and run through this again."

114

The guys stood together a few yards away, while the teacher checked mud supplies in the bucket.

Suddenly, Hodges gave a kind of bleat. "I can't take no more of this nutty stuff. I'm going to quit."

His eyes swept the group, looking for him who would deny.

"Me too," said Tuthouse. "This is clean senseless."

"Also, how about that volcano stuff again?" Jacoby wanted to know. "A person who thinks he's a volcano has got his cylinders mixed up. My dad says he knows a man where he works who thinks he's a whole earthquake, only—"

"Only what?"

"Only he's inside. Mr. Busch is out here. With us."

"Right," said Alice Hodges, tapping a forehead.

As they talked, Loren's glance had strayed away, mainly because he was sorry for Mr. Busch. He saw that the day was dark, and once again lightning flickered over the hills ominously. Well, it was probably a great method of teaching kids how to pass a super slippery football, but—

"Hey!" Hodges said abruptly. He put out a hand.

"What's up?"

"It's—why, it's raining," in an awed tone. "Real hard."

That turned out to be true; a good Carleton rain had started to fall just when innocent ranchers were least expecting it.

Mr. Busch came up about then. "Let's get started again," he suggested.

Alice didn't move. Instead, he stared at the science teacher with wide, frightened eyes. "It's begun to storm," he told him. "Can't you—can't you feel it?"

The small man glanced up. "Well, well," he said appreciatively, "it is sprinkling a trifle, isn't it? Fine, fine. Even this trifling precipitation will help us get the feel of the game."

Later on, as they drove home with the windshield

wipers chubb-chubbing, somebody said, "Did you hear what he told us about this flood?"

"Yeah," grunted Hodges. "He said it was sprinkling. Guys, what happens when it rains? I mean, a true Busch rain?"

Nobody knew right off. But Jacoby finally summed it up.

"Men," he said, "this is a bad year. Why? We read *Hamlet* and get ghosts, poisonings, and drowning in the creek. Miss Terwilliger becomes head coach, with Busch as assistant. Voters are going to decide if we consolidate with Almond Grove, and Wallace's girl goes to the drive-in all the time with our true enemy, Morgan. It's omens, guys. All bad."

And that was a fact.

CHAPTER 10 . . .

VADA LONG knew that liking Loren Wallace was a problem likely to get worse. For a time, she had thought that the Paso Verde after-game dance had solved everything, but it hadn't. Instead, it seemed to complicate whatever ailed him.

For a moment on that perfect night she'd thought he was going to kiss her, which might have helped. He'd leaned fairly close, with this agonized puppy-dog look on his face, that part she could see by moonlight. There was definitely a kiss in his eyes. A girl could tell.

Yet he hadn't; he'd got out of the car immediately and taken her into the house almost on the run. Later, after she was in bed, she'd giggled softly to herself about how funny Loren was, but now she knew truth. He wasn't a bit amusing; he was a dope. That was the tragic burden girls had to carry through life, probably—they fell in love with these complete stupes.

Oh, he'd asked her to the Football Frolic after she'd deliberately planted the suggestion about a dozen times. But she doubted that he even remembered. Besides, a girl couldn't go on forever tricking a boy into acting like a human. Sooner or later he had to take the initiative.

Nevertheless, she'd gone out of her way to talk with him whenever she could, but the effort was merely frustrating.

He'd get a vacant stare as if he couldn't stand to listen and wanted to get away. Truthfully, he seemed totally indecisive and a teeny bit loony when the situation called for decision, planning, and stability.

The Football Frolic was a big affair, that is, in a tiny way. Next to the junior-senior prom, it was the most, and like it, was formal. A boy needed to make at least a few of the preparations considered civilized. He should know the color of his girl's dress in order to get a suitable corsage, and—well, a host of things. Thus far, Loren had done nothing and gave no indication of change.

She got the enchanting picture. He would come dawdling to her house, a day or so late, and hand her a bunch of dandelions. "Picked them in my yard," he would yawn, staring over her shoulder into space. "Dandelions go with anything—even a lawn."

The prediction might not be exact, but she knew he was that kind—a dandy guy.

Thus far, his most meaningful and eloquent comment to her had been a kind of guttural noise sounding like "Uh!" although once he had said, "Nuh!" It permitted a girl to use her own imagination as to his meaning. But even that effort apparently drained him intellectually, and he might stand in silence for a full minute before a new idea came.

Yet if she had been mad at him previously, the worst came Saturday night when she'd gone to the drive-in with Bobby Morgan and Carol. She knew perfectly well he had seen her, because his car was only one row over. She would recognize that adorable little junk pile anywhere in the world. But Loren had chosen to ignore her.

When they'd left the theater, they had been right behind him. Although it wasn't good manners, she'd made Bobby blow the horn in order to attract his attention, but he'd purposely pretended she wasn't there, even when Teddy Jacoby kept turning around to look.

Vada knew a snub when she got one, and she had resolved never to speak to him again—which merely meant there would be a lot fewer "Uh's" in her life from now on.

Over the weekend, however, she reconsidered, because if he did remember, it would be awkward to go to the Football Frolic with him, talking in sign language or something. She sought the advice of a wiser head, namely her mother's. Mrs. Long's diagnosis of a girl's problems were usually frighteningly correct—because it takes one to know one, as her father often said.

She found the older woman in the living room, doing nothing in particular—reading for pleasure.

"Mother," she said, "why would a boy completely ignore a girl he was supposed to—to have a date with next Saturday night?"

Mrs. Long put down her book at once. "It would depend on which boy it was," she said thoughtfully. "Do you happen to mean Loren Wallace?"

"Yes," Vada told her. It was impossible to conceal anything around this house with a mother like that.

"In that case, it could mean anything, dear. What were the circumstances?"

Vada told her.

"Well," Mrs. Long said very seriously, "he simply might not have seen you at all. Remembering your father—or rather, having known differing types of boys, Loren's sort can look at himself in a mirror and see nothing. Why, my goodness, he can forget his own address, or that he wore a coat in freezing weather. It's a—a stage they finally get over if you give them enough time."

"But, Mother," Vada insisted, "it couldn't be that."

The older woman puzzled her fine brows. She laughed softly. "There's one other possibility," she said. "You were with Carol, but Bobby was there too. Don't you see?"

"Oh-h-h!" Vada exclaimed as light dawned. She did a

119

feathery step that made her skirt swirl; and she too giggled. "It's that, and I never would have thought of it. Oh, thank you. It explains ever so many things—"

"About Loren?"

"Uh-huh. Why, he's as clear as—as milk now. I understand him perfectly."

Mrs. Long laughed again. "You'd better tell Mrs. Wallace. I was talking with her at our bridge club and she's baffled by her son lately. She insists he's been acting just like somebody named Walter for the past week or so."

"Walter? Who's Walter?"

"That's precisely the question I asked. And do you know that Mrs. Wallace is always so poised? But mentioning Walter flustered her. She finally said he was a friend of the family—in a way." She put a finger to her lips. "I wonder how someone can be a friend of the family—in a way. Perhaps all the Wallaces are strange sometimes. Dr. Wallace is there at the hospital and—"

"Uh-huh," Vada said absently. "But what should I do now, Mom?"

"You might tell him directly."

"No. I've tried that. It doesn't work with Loren."

Her mother nodded. "It never did with your fath— It doesn't with a lot of boys. Now, let me see—"

Then she unfolded a plan, simple in design but cunning and effective.

"But—but suppose he's forgotten all about asking me to the Football Frolic?" Vada asked, sensing a flaw. "It wouldn't help a bit to have Carol there."

Mrs. Long picked up her book again—a good detective story with three satisfying murders, one especially rewarding suicide, and four near misses. It featured a romantic Peruvian detective whose clever scientific deductions in a charming accent were always being interrupted by beautiful ladies with lethal intentions.

120

"Don't you worry, dear. He won't forget," she said with supreme confidence. "Loren's type can forget to come in out of the rain, but they never, never forget to keep a date with a girl." Her dark eyes sparkled. "I happen to know."

Vada wasted no time in self-debate. She placed a telephone call to Almond Grove and talked for a few minutes with Carol, who was too tall and somewhat too free-swinging, but a redhead, and nice.

"Why not?" Carol asked richly. "What can I lose? Who is he?"

"His name is Homer Hodges," Vada told her. "He's terribly cute. I mean, he's ugly, and nice, and he despises girls. You'll like him."

"M-m-m," Carol moaned. "Interesting. It's a boy, isn't it? All right. You know me; I'll try anything twice."

It wasn't that easy with Alice Hodges, and it took Vada almost four minutes to convince him.

"A gallon of my blood, sure," the ape-man grunted, "but not none of that dance stuff. Anything else. How about two gallons?"

"Please," Vada wheedled. "For me"—which was the truth.

Finally, he gave in. "Whereat is her house?" in a beaten voice. "Also, does she know I can't dance?"

If Carol didn't know, she'd learn. "Don't be silly," she told him. "You dance fine."

"I do?"

"Of course," she told him confidently, knowing full well that after an evening with Carol he'd know how or else. That girl had muscles too, and in a battle of strong wills Vada would pick Carol over Alice any day. The work was done.

She went back to her room and examined her pretty formal. Dandelions would probably look all right, and

121

they'd be different. "I like them," she could say defiantly. "Everyone gets common orchids, but it takes imagination and—and daring to find something completely new."

Still, it wasn't dandelion season at this time of year, and shaggy chrysanthemums were not yet in bloom. So what else?

The only decorative plant doing fine in its natural ecology was poison oak, which had striking red leaves. Fortunately, she was immune. "Isn't it lovely, Mother?" she could say, pinning on a sprig. "Loren picked it himself, right out of the darkling hills."

It was an exaggeration, of course, but it expressed what a girl might expect from that awful boy.

The youth in question had indeed not forgotten the date, as Mrs. Long predicted. He remembered it only too well, and a couple of times in that final week he had even awakened from gruesome dance dreams.

They all had a similar theme. In them, he envisioned himself charging up to her house with an enormous green box under his arm, which was full of a tiny corsage. He'd push the button and great echoing gongs would beat out, announcing his utter stupidity to the world like a civil-defense warning.

Her father would come to the door. "Vada?" he'd growl in his bulldog style. "She left an hour ago with Bobby Morgan. So get lost, Wallace."

He'd do it.

On other occasions the fantasy wasn't so scary. It would be of the Almond Grove game. "The play's the thing," Coach Terwilliger would yell. "Watch it, and catch the passes of the king."

Meanwhile, out on the sidelines, Mr. Busch would be jumping around.

"No, no!" he'd scream. "More mud, Loren. Dip the ball

in the bucket and give it the double-thumb clutch. Mud! Plenty of mud."

Bad as dreams were, reality at school was worse. Politics had taken over, and the Carleton student body was split into hostile camps. Some were for consolidation and bonds; some wanted no bonds and no consolidation; a third neutral group were holding out for longer lunch periods, shorter classes, less homework, and fewer demerits. A petition got circulated for Coach Blount to please hurry up and get well. There was a rumor that the San Francisco papers were sending their ace sports reporters down whether the game was played this Saturday or a month from now.

People claimed that Carleton was the only high school in the nation with a woman as head coach, and taxpayers everywhere were interested in the name of economy. Almost anything could happen in public schools these days, some said, and the next logical step was to have a teaching machine with legs out there calling the plays. A couple of long-range prophets said the idea was already on the drawing boards, and as sure as rosebushes made little apples.

Even bigger than the game or Miss Terwilliger or special elections was the Football Frolic. Girls were apprehensive that they couldn't do the job of getting dressed in merely three or four hours, and boys were just plain nervous.

"Going to that there mad jig?" Alice Hodges wanted to know. "Got your crazy date, Wallace? I have."

Loren's jaw dropped. "You—you what?"

"Got me a woman to go with," said Hodges. "So what's funny?"

"Nothing," Loren came back. "Or at least—Say, who is she?"

He tried to think of the girl Hodges might be taking.

Somebody who wanted to live dangerously, no doubt. Alice might want her to swing through the trees, munching coconuts and cracking shells with her strong white teeth.

"You don't know her. Name's Carol. Lives in Almond Grove."

"But—"

"Don't say it," Hodges snarled. "What's wrong with Almond Grove? She wants to live there, she can, see!"

"Sure," Loren admitted.

"So all right," said Alice, mollified. "Wallace, you got one of them sliver tongues. Whyn't you say so in the first place?"

"Because I didn't think of it," Loren explained.

Hodges' reminder of that gay occasion was fairly timely, at that. He had a couple of things to do himself. From dance orientation given by his mother in the past, he realized he needed to confirm the engagement no matter what Vada had decided to do. Sure, she could have accepted a date with some other guy—Bobby Morgan or any of a half dozen other characters—but that didn't release him from the drear obligation.

If it turned out she was silly enough to go with him, he would have to know the color of her so-called dress. Merely custom. And because Carleton didn't have a flower merchant, he'd be forced to chase up to Paso Verde or down to Almond Grove and order something.

Meanwhile, he could scrape up dregs of allowance gold to pay the staggering freight. His budget was down to a dime at a time, because running a car wasn't all fun and happiness, he knew. Yet if worst came to terrible, he could always borrow from his little brother, who had a natural talent for hoarding pure money. Fred's secret bank was stuffed with unspent surpluses, mainly because he still had the young sense to ride his ten-speed bicycle to and fro.

124

Faced with dance reality that way, even so Loren had waited until Wednesday before he'd got the courage to discuss it with Vada. And then it had happened more or less by accident. He'd met her at noon out under one of the spreading live-oak trees.

Perhaps as another omen, the day was unseasonably warm and sultry, so that kids were outside of teacher range. Vada was hanging around with Shirlee Danforth and Laneva Chaffee, who were yakking their customary scintillating chatter.

It was now or never. Loren took a deep breath and walked up to those women. "Hi," he said, sort of generally.

"So it's you at last," Shirlee remarked kind of scornfully, sort of flouncing her high dudgeon. "Well, as I was saying, we have to see Miss Terwilliger, Vada. Let's go, Laneva."

"I'd say it was about time," Laneva agreed, never taking her big blue eyes off him. "By."

They went skittering away, their bright cotton skirts swishing this way and that, while they giggled like a couple of resident squirrels in a peanut factory.

"What's wrong with them?" he wanted to know, asking Vada.

She didn't answer, because who knew? Instead, "Hi, Loren," she said from far away.

He noticed she wasn't even looking at him; her eyes were what they called downcast, so he glanced down too. This year there was a true crop of acorns scattered everywhere. Once Carleton had been full of happy Indians who lived on acorns, after boiling them awhile. Now they were gone, and Loren regretted it; he liked Indians.

These days, fat woodpeckers had taken over the harvest. They drilled holes in the tree bark and planted an acorn in each one. Then they waited while a worm grew up inside each shell, and when it was ready, they came back with a fine message. That way, woodpeckers were worm farmers. It was nature's way.

"Plenty of acorns around," he ventured at last.

She looked right at him then. "My, yes," she agreed. "More than anyone realizes."

Vada said it in a creepy style, and Loren began to feel sort of like an acorn himself because she was staring at his head.

He dropped acorns and considered pigeons as an opening topic. This year a few bandtails had come back along the flyway, but maybe she didn't like pigeons. Girls seldom talked too much about wildlife; they merely acted the part.

"Uh—" he began, opening up and hoping something sensible would come out. Nothing did.

She waited. Then, "Nuh," she told him. In a way, it made a lot of sense.

Another pause.

"Loren," she said, "how's the football team?"

"Muddy," he told her, meaning it.

She glanced around, at all the dry land, probably. "You said that before," reproachfully. "You said it was muddy in the backfield. Loren, you're a—"

He hadn't expected that kind of compliment. "You're a—" he repeated inwardly. Well, he could say the same thing for her, only a lot more so.

"Thanks," he said aloud. Then he stared out over the grounds, where a breeze ruffled tree branches.

She noticed him doing it. "Isn't it pretty?" she remarked. "The leaves seem to—to dance, Loren. In the wind, I mean. Right now at the end of football season they—they literally frolic, don't they?"

They did, at that. The idea was poetic, and probably only someone like Vada could think of it. For a moment, he felt an almost unbearable inner yearning that she could really be his girl and his alone. But that was impossible. Right now, she was probably dreaming about Bobby Morgan.

126

She was leaning against the oak tree, and he noticed that a lot of mighty busy woodpeckers had been at work, stuffing acorns. Also there were ants. They were crawling up and down the tree in a regular line. Ants were interesting, once you got to know a few.

Suddenly, Vada's eyes narrowed dangerously. "Loren Wallace," she said in a smoldering voice, "do you know that the bell is going to ring in about one second?"

He nodded. She probably wanted to rush back to class and hit the books. "Yeah," in a lonesome voice. School was like that—full of inexorable bells, summoning a person.

Right there, the bell did ring; Vada Long practically stamped a foot, she was that mad. Women were irritable; the least little thing upset them.

"Oh—you!" she kind of hollered. "I—I—"

Well, sometimes a guy had to forget courtesy and throw away the book of etiquette. He broke right in.

"Are you going with me to the Football Frolic?" he had to know.

"Yes," she snapped angrily. "I am, if—"

Vada did a womanly thing. She gave him one of their exotic, mysterious glares and took off, walking fast. Man, that girl could certainly travel when the golden bells of knowledge beckoned.

Still, a few of the delicate details hadn't been settled, so he followed her and caught up after a few steps.

"Uh—" he panted, "what— at what time should I—"

She quickened her pace so they were almost running. "Eight thirty," she gasped.

People were beginning to notice, so he dropped back before he realized he'd forgotten one other item. He ran up to her again.

"Your dress?" he pleaded. "Is—?"

"Whu—" she said, "whu—"

He turned that over in his mind; these days they had a lot of colors. Federal gold, treasury gold, green, and—

He'd never heard of whu-whu, but— Maybe those pale baby orchids wouldn't do. Somewhere he'd read about green orchids, and—

"You sure? I mean, is whu-whu sort of—?" She could prefer a bunch of rosebuds.

"Of course, I'm—"

Abruptly, she stopped still and faced him, breathing hard and with her brown eyes like kindly rattlesnakes. "Loren," she said distinctly, "I think I hate you because you're the meanest, stupidest, most despicable boy in Carleton. Also, you're— Oh, I don't know!"

She'd really pinpointed the trouble, at that. "I guess," he told her. By now, a lot of people were closing in, and he didn't want to embarrass a neat girl like her by hanging around. "By," he finished.

She didn't go away. Instead, her mouth grew rosy and her eyes were brilliant. "It's a white dress, Loren," she said. "I'll be ready at eight thirty. It's on Saturday, and it's the Football Frolic. You know—after the game. Do—you —under-stand?"

"Yeah," he said.

That was a woman for a guy. True blue. With them, a date was a date even though they'd made a mistake and had to go with the stupidest person in town. Loyal? Well, some.

CHAPTER 11 . . .

IT WAS FRIDAY EVENING, and Dr. William Wallace was at home with his family. Supper was over, and he'd settled himself to read the evening *Informer* while Mrs. Wallace still busied herself in the kitchen.

That is, he was at home with most of his family. Fred was in his room, doing whatever high school freshmen did these days. But Loren had not come in yet because he was keeping an appointment with one of his teachers, a Mr. Busch. Youths these days were so frenetically busy, especially in Carleton. It seemed to Dr. Wallace that they were busier here in this one-horse—or, rather, tiny town than in the big metropolitan schools.

The man sighed and purposely ignored a front-page story in the *Informer*, going on instead to other fare. The usual brush-fire wars were going on; Congress was acting again, and the President had issued several directives here and there. He turned to the pages toward the back.

Mrs. Wallace had come into the living room. She turned on the hi-fi system to something soft, classical, and loaded with violins, picked up some needlework, and sat down.

"Uh—" Dr. Wallace asked, "did you say green?"

"Green," affirmed his wife. "They probably flew it down from San Francisco."

"No doubt," the man nodded.

He ruffled newspaper pages. "Here's an interesting filler," he said, reading slowly and with considerable wonder. "The skunk can utter a low, scolding growl when not overly excited, but he is usually silent."

"Very amusing," she said.

Dr. Wallace mulled that over in a mind. "It is somewhat odd," he admitted, more or less to himself. "One would expect the skunk to growl when he was excited, wouldn't one? But it's the other way around."

Mrs. Wallace was silent.

"Here's something else. It says that frogs and toads use their eyes to help them swallow, doing so by pulling down the eyeballs and forcing food down the throat." Dr. Wallace looked up gravely. "Think of that and then tell me that humans are peculiar."

His wife took a couple more stitches in the doily she was tatting, or whatever it was. "I've already read the paper, Bill, and since you won't discuss important things, did you notice the item about our school bond and consolidation election? We voted, you know."

"I remember," said Dr. Wallace gloomily. "And I did read the headline. I was saving the nauseating details." He scanned print. "H'm-m!" he went on. "It's about what we expected. Consolidation lost by seven votes, and the bonds fell far short of the two-thirds majority. What's unusual about that?"

There was silence while violins sobbed of the awful conditions in Vienna, probably. He went on reading. The local weatherman predicted a fifty percent chance of rain on Saturday, which was the day of the great game with Almond Grove. It might be well to take along an umbrella tomorrow when he watched his son play.

Ah, here was another item of interest among so much that was utterly boring. Twenty-six whooping cranes had arrived at the Arkansas wildlife range, exactly two less

130

than there had been the year before. Well, the tide had to turn pretty soon with whooping cranes, although bison were doing fairly well, and American Indians were coming back strong.

"Bill," said Mrs. Wallace, "I insist that we talk about our son. He worries me."

Reluctantly, he put down his paper. After a day at the hospital attending to administrative matters affecting nearly fifteen hundred loo—or, rather, mentally disturbed men, he had little left over at night to consider the aberrations of teen-agers. As far as Dr. Wallace could see, Loren was almost too normal and well-adjusted for a day and age like this. A youth had to be considered in relation to his peers, or buddies, and all of them seemed a little bit—

"What's wrong with a green orchid?" he asked impulsively. "What difference does it make?"

"It's not the orchid, Bill. I told you so before. My goodness, I wish somebody had bought me a green orchid when I was a sixteen-year-old girl."

Dr. Wallace drew himself up. "Why didn't you say so? I would have got you any color you wanted, and—"

"Bill!" said his wife. "You didn't even know me when I was sixteen. We met on—" naming the exact date, "and I was eighteen."

"That's right," a little nervously.

"It certainly is. As a matter of fact, I don't believe you ever gave me an orchid at all—until it was too late."

"Too late?"

She smiled winsomely. "I mean, until after we were married. I shouldn't have said too late. When we were going together I would have been perfectly happy with geraniums."

It was true. Lillian had been the sort of girl for whom a handful of geraniums, a ride on the streetcar, and the wonderful wide future had been enough.

131

Vistas of old romance had mellowed the man. "What do you think is wrong with Loren, then?" he asked in a kindly style, a father's way.

Mrs. Wallace shut off the music. "I really don't know. It's—it's probably only a phase in his normal maturational development, as you said in the kitchen, but—"

"But what?"

"He acts so worried."

Dr. Wallace chuckled confidently, thinking back to those years when he had been a youth—callow and weak. All that.

"Naturally he worries," he said. "Who doesn't?"

Of all the humans he had known, both in and out, the sixteen-year-old boy was often the most anxious of them all.

"But don't you think it's strange for our son to go around worrying about—about mud bushes?"

"Mud bushes?"

"Bushes of mud," confirmed Mrs. Wallace in a small, scared voice. "He mutters about them down in his room—when he thinks he's alone."

"That is odd," said the wise father. He sought logic. "Could it be *bushels* of mud? Bushels of mud makes sense. I've seen—"

"No, absolutely not. It is something to do with a bush, and with mud. Oh, and another thing—he asks the strangest questions about volcanoes. The other day he wanted to know if I thought a volcano could create rain here in Carleton. Not a 'rain' of lava, mind you. Ordinary rain. When it rains."

"Precipitation," Dr. Wallace said, clarifying the definition.

"But how could that tie in with mud bushes?" she said in the discouraged manner of mothers. "Oh, Bill, I do wish you'd have a long, heart-to-heart, father-son talk with

132

him, and—and take an interest. After all, he's only sixteen; only a little boy, although—"

"Little?" the man asked, his brows lifting. "Loren? Little?"

"I mean emotionally. You know exactly what I mean. Even grown men are—Why, you remember how you were with Walter, and—"

"All right, all right," said Dr. Wallace quickly. "Just leave that overgrown calf out of this, please. He simply strayed somewhere and hid. I had nothing to do with it. And I'll talk with Loren tonight when he comes in."

Shortly afterward, Mrs. Wallace turned the music back on while her husband considered the problem, namely Loren. For some time now, he had privately thought that everyone connected with Carleton High this year was slightly demented or getting there fast. For that matter, the entire electorate, including the public schools, showed certain signs, some of them rather ominous. Allowing the Miss Terwilliger types and ideals to take over was one of the darker symptoms. Educational disorder was here, and who knew what was likely to happen next.

He had been strongly against allowing the English teacher to interfere with the athletic program, because it could have far-reaching psychological ill effects. To be sure, she was only filling in temporarily for Coach Blount, but whatever the expediency, she wasn't helping the team build their life image of womankind as the eternal feminine.

It hadn't been his place to protest. Besides, a number of citizens in Carleton had raised the question immediately, but somehow they had been overruled. With the football season over tomorrow night, the damage had been done.

A Miss Terwilliger syndrome was to be expected, but these other elements—mud bushes and volcanoes—were a puzzle in considering Loren's mental state.

Unless—Yes, now he had a clue. One of the lad's teachers was named Busch. Perhaps the term "mud" applied to him. High school youngsters had a way of inventing endearing names for their teachers.

For some obscure reason, Mr. Busch's name was mud with his students. Yet the few times he had had occasion to speak with the science teacher, the man had seemed a decent sort who was genuinely interested in his work. The nickname must refer to a certain opacity in his teaching, like the expression "as clear as—"

" 'Mud' Busch," Dr. Wallace said in his mind, confessing to some amusement. He had done a little teaching himself, and in one particular year had dwelt at length on Eskimo culture to a class in anthropology. From then on he had been known as Walrus Wallace, although his students had meant no real disrespect.

" 'Mud' Busch," he said to himself again. In his time, the buddies had come up with saltier names for their dear teachers.

"Bill!" said Mrs. Wallace in an alarmed tone. "Now you're doing it too."

Dr. Wallace realized he had spoken aloud without intending to do so. It was stress, of course. People of every degree were being subjected to that in modern times. Some were climbing the walls to get out; others were struggling like crazy to get in—or so it seemed.

"Sorry," he said. "I was thinking aloud, I suppose. Perhaps Loren is—"

Suddenly, he snapped his fingers. "Volcanoes!" he exclaimed. "They could have something to do with mud. It seems to me that I did read about a chap in Washington, or possibly at one of the universities, who has this volcanic theory of weather. Yes, I recall it now. This man believes that vast quantities of volcanic ash spewed into the atmosphere absorb solar radiation, and—"

134

"Bill, there aren't any volcanoes here. This is Carleton."

"Of course," replied her husband. "All I was saying is that I'm sure there is a logical explanation for whatever Loren is saying. He has some legitimate reason for discussing bushes, volcanoes, and mud. I suppose we'll know what that is soon enough. But it's not his mind, Lillian. Loren's mind is as sound as a—" He almost said "dollar," but that wouldn't do at all. "He's normal, dear. Perfectly normal. Nothing is wrong with him at all—except boyhood."

At that precise moment, Loren did have a logical association with pure mud. Mr. Busch had called another secret practice behind his house out of town. This time he concentrated on receiving the pass after it had been deflected in flight by his spraying the ball with the full blast of a garden hose. He'd stuck out a few luau torches so a guy could see a little and also get seen.

Going over there, Jacoby had said: "Guys, Busch may really know something. Did you see the paper?"

Everyone had, because who missed the comics? Also they read the results of the special school election.

"Why?" asked Hodges.

"It said there was a fifty percent chance of rain tomorrow. Busch had us practicing in mud, so he's at least half right."

Tuthouse was scornful. "So it does rain a little," he said, "what does that do? The whole field is grass, Jacoby. Remember when we played Valley City last year? It rained and got us wet, but there wasn't any of this soupy mud Busch likes."

Teddy shrugged. "That's so," he nodded, "but how did he know so long in advance that it was likely to rain on Saturday?"

"Simple," snorted Alice.

"What do you mean, simple?"

"Merely volcanoes," Hodges announced. "You get as nutty as Busch; then you go on from there until this here idiot like you, Jacoby, claims it's right. Me, I ain't going out for football no more. I'm going to take archery or something."

"Here too," said Tuthouse. "With Miss Terwilliger running the team and Busch dipping us guys in mud, secretly, I know one thing for sure. There's something rotten in the town of Carleton."

Mr. Busch, however, was delighted with the practice. Loren would toss the slippery ball and Mr. Busch would run along, knocking it off course with the garden hose. Even so, Hodges and Jacoby got good at catching it. As the science teacher explained, in full mud conditions the ends were to go out wide when Tuthouse called the play. Hodges and Teddy were to sift through the line for the passes.

Loren felt sorry for Mr. Busch, until they had cleaned up and Mrs. Busch made them sit down and eat home-baked cookies and ice cream. For a woman that old, around thirty-five, she was all right. Both she and her husband talked to them in a friendly style that made a guy feel that his sayings were important. The science teacher couldn't be completely daft.

Also he told them some good news. "I've heard that Coach Blount is going to be on the bench tomorrow," he said. "At least for a little while."

When they were back in the car and headed home, Alice spoke for everyone. "You heard, didn't you? Blount'll be back. Know what that means? Guys, we go back to normal. When Blount sees how they done his good team while he's been gone, why, he'll take over and call the plays from the bench."

"Sanity, your name is human," Jacoby said, breathing a sigh of relief. "But I'll never forget how close they came to getting us youths, even after I graduate."

"If you graduate," Tuthouse added.

"Yeah," Alice had to say. "If."

When Loren reached home, Fred had tuned in a great television serial that was realistic and in touch with the times. It was about a detail of cops in a big-city force who went around stamping out juvenile crime and making kids respect the badge.

Usually, the youngest cop got right in there and mingled with the gang until he won confidence. He'd find out when the next big rumble was going to be pulled, so the squad could close in at the right time. Sure, they might have to gun down a couple of the vicious leaders, but after they had healed up, they gave them a lot of fine advice in little talks. Next thing people knew, the same gang would be urging other tough kids to go down to the rec hall and become good citizens. It worked nearly every time on the show, except once when the cops had to kill a delinquent, so naturally he couldn't hear the lecture.

Loren would have liked to listen, but he was so weak from mud-slinging weakness that after he'd eaten supper he went back to his room to hit the sack.

He was there only a minute when there was a rap on his door. It turned out to be his dad.

"Come in," he said.

Dr. Wallace entered and took a chair, where he sort of slumped down and let his eyes roam around the place. Loren looked too; there wasn't anything here that belonged to a father. He had borrowed a necktie last June, but he distinctly remembered giving it back. Who wanted a necktie?

Finally, "How's the team?"

"Not so good, Dad," Loren said in an exploratory tone. Something was up.

"We always say 'as good as can be expected,' Loren."

"That's about it."

Sure enough, his dad came right to the point. "Your

137

mother tells me you've been talking about bushes and volcanoes. Do they have any special meaning?"

"Yes," said Loren, "but I can't tell you."

"Why not?"

"I promised I wouldn't. It's a secret until after to-morrow."

Dr. Wallace thought that over. "All right, we'll find out tomorrow. Mind if I ask one more question?"

"No."

"Why did you buy a green orchid?"

Loren flushed. "It was the only one they had left."

"Fair enough," his dad said, getting up and putting his hand on the door latch. "By the way, how's 'Mud' Busch, your science teacher, these days?"

"You mean Mr. Busch?" Loren asked, surprised.

"Sure. Old 'Mud,' as he's called."

Loren had to blink, and it hit him that Jacoby was right. Everything was going over the brink. "Oh, he's fine, Dad," he said, humoring a sick father. " 'Mud' Busch is just great."

Afterward, he worried. Daffiness could hit Carleton High School, Miss Terwilliger, Mr. Busch, Hamlet, and the whole town. But when it was beginning to get his dad, it was hitting mighty close. He'd been working too hard, probably, and could use a rest.

Just before he went to sleep, Loren wondered whether he should have a talk with his mother. But he let it go. Maybe she was on the brink herself, and no use to worry her.

CHAPTER 12...

SATURDAY MORNING FINALLY DAWNED, and Loren was glad. By this time tomorrow, he figured, everything would be over—the Almond Grove game, his date with Vada Long, the whole mess. Stuff would settle back to merely miserable.

Sure, he was tense, but he had to expect that, and it could be worse. For example, some people might be anxious about how a game was going to come out, but a Carleton player never needed to give it a thought. He already knew.

As for Vada, Loren knew about her too. She was Morgan's steady girl, but too nice to turn down some youth who happened to ask her to go to the Football Frolic. He'd get her tonight, jig around awhile, go home, and hit the sack. Afterward, she could hate him all she wanted.

Still, Loren had these daydreams, no matter how hard he tried to fight them off. While he was getting dressed, something clicked in his mind, and he saw the field of battle in his imagination.

"Wallace has passed for the third Carleton touchdown," the public-address system was blatting out. "Now he's fading back to try again. There's the pass —a long, long one. It's good; it's completed to Jacoby and Carleton has tied the game! Folks, if Carleton can hang on now, it means that Coach Tom Blount's Valley City team will win the league."

Later—in the dream, naturally—he was holding Vada Long in confident arms. "You were marvelous," she was whispering. "You were—"

"Loren!"

It was his mother calling him for breakfast, and the dream evaporated like windshield mist when the heat was on. He got out there fast because he was starved, but also because his mother meant right now at mealtime. He noticed that his dad was already gone.

After a few waffles and stuff, Loren came up for air and looked around. He could see the whole horizon outside through the big floor-length dinette window and just as he looked the sun got lost in a huge bank of clouds. They were pushing in over the Santa Lucias from the ocean twenty miles beyond. The weatherman had been right; there probably was a fifty percent chance for rain. Around here, clouds like that could do it if they tried.

He downed a couple more waffles and looked again. This time there was a yellowish cast to the sky which gave everything down here a peculiar sickly glow. It would probably clear up before this afternoon. It always did at this season.

Fred had to get in the word. "Raining up in San Francisco," the kid offered in that wise style he was using—merely a passing phase. Loren had been through it himself back when he was young. "Also in Oakland. Heard it on the radio. They said this was the tail end of something like a girl's name—Katherine, or Ophelia. Forget which."

"Sure, sure," Loren told him absently. It was only a stage; all kids got it for a while.

He turned to his mother. "How's Dad this morning?" he asked cautiously. No need to worry her.

"Why, he's fine," said Mrs. Wallace from where she presided over the waffle iron. "Why? Why do you ask, Loren?"

140

Before answering, he finished a few slices of bacon he'd started. Around the home, his parents liked one thing at a time in a guy's mouth.

"Wondering, was all," he said evasively. "He—he was in my room talking to me last night, and—"

"I know. Another glass of milk, dear?"

He thought it over. "No, thank you," he said. He'd already had a couple, and besides, his appetite was puny, probably because he had got fired up about the game.

"Did your father—" Mrs. Wallace began. But then she let it drop. "Never mind, Loren," she went on. "You have a big day ahead of you, with the game and dance. We'll talk it over later, the three of us."

Loren blinked a couple of times. So she'd been noticing it too about his dad.

"All right, Mom," he told her. "And don't worry. We'll make it through." One thing he knew, if the head of the house was sick, everyone would get behind him.

"I won't," she said.

Mrs. Wallace had been right about it's being a big day, but how big it would be nobody knew—at least with one possible exception. Afterward, there was speculation about him, because how could understanding a volcano help a teacher make a prophecy? It couldn't, nearly everyone claimed.

Loren fooled around home the rest of the morning, had lunch, and went over to see a few of the guys who were at Jacoby's house. By that time, the heavy clouds had covered the whole sky, but nothing had happened. Overcast was common at this time of year.

Hodges had it straight that Coach Blount would be at the game. "He was by our house," Alice said. "Told my dad. He don't look none too healthy, but he'll be there. And know what? Blount thinks it's funny that Miss Terwilliger is our head coach. He even laughed."

Jacoby nodded. "It's what's called gallows' humor," he

141

said knowingly. "Anything really gruesome is funny to some people."

"I'm glad he'll be there, no matter what makes him laugh," Tuthouse put in.

Joe Martinez grinned. "The coach won't see anything funny after the game gets going," he offered. "I hear Almond Grove is going to start their fourth string against us and let everybody get in game time. And if Blount hears what Busch has been doing—" Joe made a slicing motion across his throat, but he didn't say anything more. He'd been let in on the mud secret, but with Martinez it was as safe as if it was locked up inside a social studies book.

Finally the moment came to get over to the gym and suit up, so they all piled into Loren's car and went there. Sure enough, Mr. Busch and Miss Terwilliger were waiting outside, and she gave them a little talk. It was about how Carleton should fight hard but clean and use sportsmanship all the time.

"The die is cast," she finished. "Nothing can change the outcome but how the game is played." Wise words.

Her eyes were sort of flashing around while she spoke, and the wind was whipping her skirt. Meanwhile, Mr. Busch stood in the background saying nothing, and the team kept watching the ground.

About this time, the Almond Grove buses began to arrive, and Loren glanced up to see if they were going in the right direction. He noticed Mr. Busch staring out over the field.

The science teacher was looking at the mountains instead of at Miss Terwilliger, so Loren did too. The hills were a kind of luminous dark green, and the massed clouds had turned black. Down through them stabbed three bright cracks of lightning that reflected and showed the depth of the sky. A faint grumble followed.

"Loren!" a voice snaked out. "Pay attention."

He jumped a little.

"Yes, Coach," he said.

"Go in the gym with Mr. Busch," ordered the English teacher, "and when you come out on the field, I want you to show Coach Blount that we haven't all been idle." Her eyes strayed to Mr. Busch. "Of course, some of us have."

After that, the team trotted inside, because Miss Terwilliger liked to see a youth get in and move briskly. The last thing Loren saw was people headed for the bleachers —Almond Grove rooters, cheerleaders, pompon girls. All that.

"Wallace," Teddy Jacoby asked when they were at the lockers, "notice the weather? It's yellow, kind of. It's like that saying from *Hamlet* about the moist star being sick with eclipse. Everything looks sick. I don't like it."

Loren remembered the line because he had read it when he was Horatio. It went, "The moist star, upon whose influence Neptune's empire stands, was sick almost to doomsday with eclipse." At that, it about wrapped up the Carleton situation.

But no time for philosophy. Miss Terwilliger's talk had taken so long that a couple of the team weren't even dressed all the way when they got the signal to get out on the field. Jerry Parsons and Bugatti were still stuffing jerseys and lacing pants as they hobbled out.

There was an overflow crowd by now, with bleachers filled and plenty of unpaid admissions from grammar school and town hanging around sidelines. Three or four friendly dogs had come to see the game too. The Almond Grove rooting section looked good with its massed colors of orange and black.

When the Carleton team took the field, a mighty squeak came from forty-two loyal girls who shook fierce pompons to the angry sky. Following Terwilliger instructions, the team first went over to the bench to pay homage, as she called it, to Coach Blount. Nobody knew what homage meant, so the guys merely said, "Hello."

He was huddled in a blanket, even though he had on a big woolly overcoat, and he looked plenty undernourished. Yet he had the same old smile on his granite-type face. Miss Terwilliger sat beside him.

"Hodges," said the coach, "and Tuthouse, Jacoby, and you, Wallace. I hear you're the first-string backfield." He grinned.

"Yeah, Coach," Alice answered in a husky voice. "And are we glad to see you."

"The four horsemen," Blount said, "of the Augean stables." Man, he had a sense of the ridiculous.

Everyone went back to the Carleton end of the field and began to warm up.

Out there, Jacoby pointed. "What'd I tell you, Loren?" he yelled. "Notice across the field near the Almond Grove coaches? Reporters, and a photographer. I heard they were coming down from San Francisco, but I couldn't believe it."

It was true. A little later on, Loren saw them over talking with Coach Terwilliger and taking a couple of pictures. She made a real photographic study that way, blowing her whistle.

At last it got to be game time. Carleton won the toss, and Jacoby decided to kick. The officials shooed everybody off the field when the ball got placed. But somebody overlooked a big black dog who tore out and nuzzled the ball until it fell over. Alice Hodges was going to complain about something like that happening to get Carleton off balance, but he didn't.

"Hey," he said, "keep quiet, guys. Just happened to remember that's my own dog."

"Omens," Jacoby had to say. "We got a million. Something's going to happen, sure."

It did. Almond Grove hadn't started its fourth string after all. Mr. Manchester, their coach, had probably de-

144

cided to close in for the kill right away. Bobby Morgan was in, along with most of their first-string guys.

Alice got away a good kick that went out of bounds on their 20-yard line. Then they took over. Morgan made a first down on a line buck, and Hammond went around left end for another. Each time Loren picked himself up after the play, he felt as if a herd of insane hippos had trampled down his spine the full length.

It wasn't hard to figure Almond Grove strategy: pure power. They scored their first touchdown in eight plays, mainly right through the line and over Loren Wallace.

Their second score came almost immediately afterward. Hodges had taken the kickoff for a good return to their 40. Jacoby called Coach Terwilliger's secret play, the "To be, or not to be." It turned out not. All four backfield men handled the ball fine, but by that time the whole Almond Grove team had rushed in. Loren scuttled back to toss the pass away, but Ojeda intercepted and ran the full distance. Morgan converted, naturally.

The rest of the first quarter was normal, ending with a score of 27 to 0, and it looked as if Morgan's prediction would come out true: this year, Almond Grove was going to break a hundred.

During the rest period, the Carleton song girls whipped up team spirit by singing the fight song.

It went:

"The rainbow comes down in Carleton,
Nestled close to the mountains high.
There's a school that is worth
All the wealth of the earth
And for her I'll live or die."

A lump came into Loren's throat when he heard those stirring words. A lot of the guys here today were probably going to do it; die, that was. As for himself, he guessed he

145

was getting off lucky because he had only a broken clavicle. It wasn't so much, and a person had only one clavicle to give to his beloved school, but it could be a surprise to his parents.

Thinking about them, he glanced into the bleachers and saw his dad. Dr. Wallace had an umbrella with him, a big black job which he'd opened already. Well, every family had its peculiar personalities, a son supposed. Live, and let live.

The Carleton manager had run out with those little bottles to slake a guy's thirst, but it turned out that it wasn't the regular freshman who usually did the job.

Jacoby, who was lying beside Loren with his face in the kindly dirt, looked up. "It's Busch," he said. Suddenly he put out an inquiring paw and stood up. "Wallace," he yelped, "told you so. It's raining."

Before Loren could answer, the science teacher was there, bending down. He had a kind of diabolical grin; that was the only way to describe it.

"Now," he whispered, "you boys remember what I've told you. Keep the ball in your possession as much as you can. But don't be afraid to pass, and watch for fumbles. I think it may rain a little."

Even afterward, even when Mr. Busch had gone to Hawaii on his new job, guys around Carleton were destined to use that phrase whenever the climate changed. As it was, a few of them even began to believe in the Busch theory of volcanoes.

Of course, Carleton wasn't the only place in California that got it. Seven inches of rain fell in San Francisco; the Oregon coast was ripped by winds that finally battered Vancouver and howled out to sea toward the Orient where they came from. The regular weathermen had goofed, apparently, because who could expect even the tail end of a typhoon in sunny California?

146

The second quarter went about as people expect in an ordinary Carleton rainstorm. Everything bogged down, and there were plenty of fumbles. Yet there wasn't so much rain as wind, which drove the stuff in horizontally. Spectators without fever interest in football began to leave, and Coach Blount was hurried into a car and driven home.

Almond Grove had sent in a mixture of its second and third strings, so nobody scored, and there was a lot of trampling and grunting at midfield. Passes tossed into the wind either missed or were batted down.

"What a storm!" Jacoby yelled in Loren's ear. "Busch was right. They're only going to beat us by three or four more touchdowns in this weather."

Could be.

The half ended and the rooting sections went into their act, waving soggy pompons and screaming yells. The band music came in gusts caught on the wind, whipped along, or lost entirely. Most of the adults had gone home, but kids and teachers stayed. They couldn't get much wetter, so why not?

Both teams went into locker rooms because it was blowing so hard, although the rain had let up a little. As they passed the Almond Grove bench, Loren saw Miss Terwilliger and Mr. Hipper sort of hollering at the opponent's coaches.

She was waving arms and vigorously shaking her head no. As it developed later, the Almond Grove principal had suggested that the game be declared over, the weather being unsuited to sport, with the score staying as it was. Mr. Hipper was agreeable; he was sneezing and shaking his head yes.

But they hadn't reckoned with Carleton's fine old English teacher. "No," she'd declared, "absolutely not."

She had given them a lecture about how in this day of

147

hard-subject education, adults shouldn't set an example of softness and be quitters. There was this gentle rain falling like mercy, and to stop a scheduled football game because of a little water was sheer nonsense and timidity.

As if to back her up, the rain grew less, although the wind kept up, and Almond Grove mentors got the message. The game would go on.

When the teams returned to the field there had been a change, Loren noticed. The lightning up in the hills was frantic, and the air had turned warmer.

Also, there was another difference. Almond Grove had sent in its full first team—the league champs, for sure. There they were, the whole tough outfit from Morgan to Rhino Serra, a two- or three-hundred-pound back certain to make all-state. Maybe Miss Terwilliger's ideas had taught their coach a good lesson or something.

Loren heard someone calling his name, and he glanced over to the sidelines. Opposite him, on the 20-yard line, was Mr. Busch.

"Now, Loren," he yelled, "take it away."

Or so it seemed. But it could have been "take Loren away"—he didn't know.

Larry Vance raised his arm to signal the Almond Grove kickoff, and it was just as if he'd reached up and pulled a lever. The wind throttled down, and as their team surged forward the true rains came.

It was a Busch rain. The ball, already in the air, hit the first genuine downpour and stopped almost dead in midair, tumbling into Joe Martinez' hands. He made two yards, slipped, but hung on.

In the huddle, Loren saw the drops bouncing off Jacoby's helmet like popcorn.

"Teddy," he hollered, trying to talk without opening a mouth too wide because who wanted to drown out here on land. "Look down."

"Why?" yelling.

"Try it."

Jacoby did. He bent over and scooped up a handful of what had been soggy dirt before. It oozed through his fingers like a good grade of bean soup. "Mud!" he spluttered. "Busch mud."

Somebody saw Miss Terwilliger jumping up and down at the bench and waving a signal. Jacoby called time out while she sent in Billy Dade for Jo-Jo Maller in the line, which was a surprise. Billy was so weak that once he squatted down he could scarcely get up unaided.

He had a message. "Ol' Lady Terwilliger wants you should stick to line play. Don't try any passes in this muck."

"O. K.," burbled Jacoby through a mouthful of rain. His not to reason why.

Lardboy dutifully called the plays. Teddy tried an end run and lost five. Hodges lost two off right tackle, mainly by bouncing back.

In the huddle again, Jacoby said: "Guys, the ball feels just like it did in our special practice. Lardboy, you call a pass whether Coach Terwilliger likes it or not."

As if to emphasize the idea, a big snake of lightning struck close, with the blast of thunder right with it. As play resumed, Loren felt the soggy ball squish into his hands. The Carleton ends had gone wide, sucking out plenty of Almond Grove guys to cover them. Jacoby and Hodges had sneaked through the line and were out there. He gave the ball the Busch double-thumb lock, picked Hodges as most in the open, and fired one. It slogged through the air like a wounded buzzard, dripping mud, and Alice clasped it to a broad stomach in hoops of steel. The pass was good for twenty yards and a first down.

Five plays and five passes later, the mighty Carleton mud hens were over the line for their first touchdown.

Later, of course, everyone in town said that if the sport of mud polo could be substituted for eleven-man football, the team was certain to take the state title. But that was when the whole astonishing performance was over.

While it was going on, those who stayed to watch, such as Dr. Wallace, who wanted to know more about his son's mental health, could hardly believe what they saw.

Almond Grove couldn't hang on to the ball. Sure, they ripped off some fine gains now and then. But usually, the thing squirted out of their hands before they could get into the clear.

Meanwhile, mud had made Carleton's finest hour—except that Jacoby needed to orient his team about which way they were going. Billy Dade, especially, kept getting lost in the Almond Grove line.

Somebody tried to switch on the arcs for better light, but the power was gone because of the storm, and it wouldn't have made much difference anyway. By now, the whole field was one big lake of pure mud, with the water standing a couple of inches deep everywhere.

That didn't hinder the mud hens as Busch training paid off. While Almond Grove beef slowed down, slipped, and stumbled, the Carleton backfield grew nimbler and more sure of itself.

In all, Loren had thrown twenty-seven passes and completed twenty-two of them as the game moved into the final minutes. They'd put across one more touchdown, then another, passing for all three conversions to move the score to 27–21.

That was how it would end, Loren knew—with Almond Grove out in front by one touchdown—and it was just as well. It took the edge out of the game if a person needed a typhoon to humble the league champs.

There was time for a couple more plays, and Carleton had the ball. "Try a long one, Tuthouse," Jacoby screamed.

150

"Call it. Run back, Loren, and pitch a long one out to me."

Then he had to go hunt up Billy Dade again, but he'd found a quick way. If there were twelve guys on the Almond Grove team, one of them had to be Billy.

Here came the play. Tuthouse took the hand-off and tossed it back while Jacoby slogged forward. Loren drifted farther behind. It was fairly difficult to tell which guy was which now, but he saw a bundle of mud running out there. The guy turned and put up a hand, so he guessed it could be Jacoby as well as anyone. He pitched out, and the ball soared upward in a muddy arc.

It was good. Teddy scooped it in and crossed the goal line standing up, to tie the score. But Morgan batted down the pass for conversion.

Somebody shot the final gun, and a few people heard it. The game was over. But before anyone could get off the field, Mr. Hipper's voice splatted over the public-address system.

"The Football Frolic," he sort of barked, like a seal coming up for air, "is canceled." People could tell he meant it. "Go home," he yelled, "and get dry."

Then he sneezed. Amplified that way, it was the king-size sneeze of all time, representing the largest cold in existence, probably, loud as thunder and as big as all outdoors, as they said.

"Tiger" Terwilliger's team had come through.

CHAPTER 13 . . .

IT WAS SATURDAY EVENING a week later. Loren stood in front of a mirror and tried again. He'd started early enough so he had plenty of time to practice, a method he'd learned from Mr. Busch.

Still, this necktie kept coming out wrong. Either the front part was about a foot too long, or the back part hung down three or four inches. Also his shirt kept strangling him, and he'd nicked himself twice while shaving. That was a fairly high accident average, because on the side he'd done it on he had only nine real whiskers.

Well, no matter how this evening turned out—horrible, or merely awful—this had been a week. The first thing Carleton had had to do was dig out from the mud in city streets.

The school board had met in emergency session right after the game and abandoned eleven-man football forever, no matter what else happened. Mr. Hipper had forced the issue in his kindly style; he'd turned in his resignation orally, kind of hollering it into the storm pending the board's decision. It was an ultimatum, as they called it: either Carleton got out of football, or he would get out of Carleton.

As Loren got it, the principal had come out against any kind of football at all, six-man, touch, or rugby. He claimed youths got injured or contracted pneumonia in the game under the best conditions, and under the worst —the kind they had around here—no telling what could happen.

Also, he'd kept the whole story out of the newspapers by insisting that the team hadn't really been coached by Miss Terwilliger, because Coach Blount was there for anybody to see. Also he'd yelled that obviously nobody had coached this team. Besides saying he would sue anyone who printed such a story, Mr. Hipper had claimed he'd get in there and do something violent right now, like breaking a reporter's pencils. He didn't like the press too well.

Whatever it was, the reporters left at half time under the impression that the game had been called off. But some people thought it was because the photographer hadn't brought his underwater camera with him.

Almond Grove was pretty mad. Some incompetent observers said that Mr. J. Edward Pauley, their principal, had met informally with Mr. Hipper in front of the public-address system. Mr. Pauley said that the proposed consolidation of the two schools should be postponed indefinitely, if not for all time. He doubted that anyone from Carleton would be too happy at his school for at least a full generation.

Mr. Hipper was reported to have taken considerable umbrage and told Mr. Pauley that as far as he was concerned, Almond Grove could go consolidate with the other nuts in Del Obispo County. Then he'd sneezed some more into the public-address system—which wasn't like Mr. Hipper at all.

Yet who could blame Almond Grove? They had the best team in the league, and to tie a dinky little place like Carleton ruined their record and gave the championship to Valley City.

There was a lot of debate about whether football should

stay. If games got scheduled next season at the same time as major earthquakes, regular national emergencies, tornadoes, and epidemics, the chances were strong that Carleton might even get out of the cellar. Finally, through board compromise and consultations with the new state department of education, the school got admitted to the six-man league.

Also, Mr. Busch had been acting funny. Teddy Jacoby put up his hand in class and asked whether he would explain his volcano theory of weather prediction, but the science teacher had demurred.

"I'd rather not, Teddy," he'd explained with a strange little smile. "Perhaps some other time, but not now."

He'd even taken down his anemometer, rain gauges, and stuff from the roof.

Loren knew why. Merchants in town might ask the reason he didn't give them mud practice too. It wouldn't make for good parent-teacher relationships if they knew Mr. Busch realized a typhoon was coming and kept quiet.

Alice Hodges had his own ideas. "Like nobody would have believed him," he'd snorted. "Guys, we didn't. Why should they?"

The mud-hen backfield held their silence, because Mr. Busch got word he had a job in Hilo, Hawaii, at the end of the semester. He'd already asked Mr. Hipper for a contract release, and the principal was doing his best to find a replacement. Hodges said his dad knew the man's policy. If a teacher could better himself and get out of Carleton while the getting was good, he bent over backward to help.

The biggest surprise was the new Football Frolic. It hadn't been canceled after all. Miss Terwilliger had gone storming into Mr. Hipper's office on Monday and demanded that the dance be held this Saturday, even though it did overlap into basketball season. The func-

154

tion had been a tradition at Carleton for three principals back that she knew of, the English teacher claimed, and she didn't see how a newcomer had the right to change it.

Also, nearly every Carleton mother called up with the same message, guys waiting in the office to be judged maintained. Most of them said the same thing—that Mr. Hipper couldn't possibly understand. Their daughters had their pretty dresses all ready and expectations whetted, and not going was damaging to home, school, and community. Some mothers said that being taken to a formal dance was an education in itself and probably the high point in a girl's entire life. That way, it was almost as important as phonics in reading, and other stuff in basic training.

Gradually, Mr. Hipper understood. By Monday afternoon, the notice went around, and naturally girls squealed in glee, and guys looked stunned. Also there were a few groans here and there, because in a whole week social lines at Carleton had been shifted around. Last week's date was this week's hate.

Whatever else, it had taught Loren a fine lesson: never buy an orchid, because that flower didn't stand up too well even under refrigeration. It had got wilted around the edges, so he'd had to go back to Oak Hills and get some little roses.

Other than that, things settled down. Miss Terwilliger acted as if she'd never coached a football team in her life and didn't intend to try. The class merely finished reading *Hamlet* and taking a lot of tests about it. Sure enough, that "sweet prince," as they called him, should have taken the advice of his elders and gone back to school in Wittenburg right at the start. Why? Because everyone in the play except one guy named Fortinbras died from poisoning. Being in school would probably have been better, although who knew what Wittenburg was like until he went there?

Right now, Loren took another loop on the necktie, straining forward for a better view. This time, the whole works dropped into place, and both ends came out even with only a half inch or so hanging down. Perfection.

So he was ready. For the last time he checked details—allowance gold, handkerchief, comb, and so on. He straightened his sagging shoulders and went out to face the music like a—well, man.

They were waiting in the living room—his parents and Fred. But there was nothing to worry him there. His dad hadn't flipped, after all. It was only a misunderstanding caused by his going around the house and talking to himself about secret mud practice. Confusion.

For an instant, he considered taking along both corsages and letting that girl choose for herself between a faded green orchid of yesterday, and baby roses. But according to his mother, fresh flowers, no matter how ordinary, were better than elegant old ones. And she should know. After all, mothers were women.

"By," he told them from the doorway.

Mrs. Wallace was up beside him, picking something off his formal sports coat. A flaw, maybe. "My big boy," she said with her eyes shining in a nutty style. But he didn't mind; a son got used to it after a while.

He got out of there.

Loren had already spent practically a whole afternoon sweeping out the car and polishing it. In this darkness it didn't look half bad, maybe only a quarter. But it took him a while to start it in this cold weather.

He drove through Carleton's business district—four stores and a filling station, over the Salinas bridge, and out along the river road to Vada Long's place.

It wasn't until he reached the gate and stopped to unlatch it that he remembered he hadn't checked again with her to find out if she still wanted to go.

Maybe she'd changed her mind, but that was her business. Nobody could figure them. As he drove down the circling driveway to her house, he saw a dark shape out on the lawn that looked vaguely familiar. But that was impossible; he didn't know any animals that big.

Loren stopped fairly near the house and went up to the door. Mr. Long answered the chimes. He was a big man, deep-tanned, who wore a moustache and took it seriously. "Oh, it's you," he snarled in a kindly style, turning inward. "Here's Loren. Come in."

Mrs. Long was there, a neat, slim woman who looked as if being Vada's mother hadn't taken too much heartbreak. She seemed willing for him to be there and even asked that he sit down, which he did, holding the corsage box in one paw.

"That was quite a game last Saturday," Mr. Long began, "although—"

But they wouldn't let the head of the household make conversation. Vada came in, and she and Mrs. Long took over completely.

Maybe it was lucky, because he was practically speechless. If he'd thought she was all right before, he wasn't prepared for this. They'd done something to her with their crazy woman-witchery. Her hair was different, and she looked sophisticated. That is, she made him feel he was a lot younger, say around ten years old and awkward as snowshoes. Her dress had a kind of off-the-shoulder cut that could mean she'd catch a bad cold if she wasn't careful. Also her shoes glittered.

"Hi, Loren," she said in a new voice—sort of grave and formal. "Have you met my father? Father, this is Loren Wallace."

"We've already met," Mr. Long told her, which was true.

Loren remembered the box and held it out, saying, "Uh—this is—"

"For me? Really?" Vada yakked in these cultivated tones. She tore into the tissue paper, located the baby roses, which weren't bad, and held them up to her dress for her mother to see. At that, they went fairly well with the color. White. A rose was dependable.

They hung around there awhile longer—about two minutes—while he helped her into the coat thing she had, mainly with getting the right arms in each side. Then they took off while Mr. and Mrs. Long stood in the doorway, keeping an eye on their daughter as long as they could, probably. He made a slow start with his car to reassure them that he wasn't a hot rodder; old people couldn't tell a dog from a bomb. They got scared even when a guy was driving something that could hardly get out of low gear.

He expected her to start in yakking like mad the way women did around school, but she didn't say a word, so he settled down to driving. It probably did a woman good to be quiet once in a while.

Still, he felt her presence here in the car almost more eloquently than when she talked. Once he turned and looked at her, glancing back fast because she was staring right at him in a dreamy style. But he got into reality. She was Morgan's girl, and he didn't need to worry about her at all, because tomorrow she'd return to her one true love, naturally.

"Loren—"

He thought she'd spoken his name. "Yeah?" he asked. "I mean, yes, you spoke?"

"I was so frightened last Saturday with you out there in that—"

"Merely mud," he told her.

"You were wonderful," she said.

For a second, he thought he'd explain what had happened—all about Busch and volcanoes. But that was too complicated. Anyway, if a guy needed mud to shine, he was badly off.

158

He noticed that there was a thin moon tonight and a sky full of stars—a broad band of those hugging down close. There wasn't going to be a hurricane to pull him out of this Football Frolic fiasco; he'd have to go it alone.

Suddenly, Vada said, "Oh!" in a scared little voice.

He put on the brakes automatically. A stray cow had walked into the swoop of headlights and then turned away to munch roadside grass.

"I'm sorry," softly.

He noticed that she'd touched his arm and moved closer to him. "That's all right," he told her gruffly.

"I—I was startled," she explained, taking away her hand and leaving a spot that burned with—well, something. "For a second I thought it was Henry. We could have hurt him."

She was right. Hitting that animal could leave a scratch. Of course, it would total out Loren's car.

"Henry?" he asked. "Who's Henry?"

Now she giggled. "It's a pet we have at home. A sort of —well, a pet bull. Oh, I know it's silly, but—"

He had to nod. Nothing was sillier, he could agree, remembering Walter. But everyone had to learn, he supposed, so no use to try to tell Vada that anybody who made a pet out of that kind of animal was in for a fine disappointment.

Instead, he killed a smooth, careful right, topped the hill, and there was good old Carleton High emblazoned by four or five lights.

They reached the parking lot, and he located a good place where they could dig out ahead of the mob when this fascination ended. When he got out to open the door for Vada, he could hear their insane strings at this distance. They must have the same wizards of fretboard and vacuum tube—almost no music, sure, but plenty of the genuine panther rhythm. In fact, that combo was almost pure beat, twice as fast as the human heart.

Different couples were already straggling in, he saw. He would have hated to take this alone.

From somewhere in the darkness, a voice bawled, "Hey, Wallace, that you?"

Jacoby.

"It's me," he replied.

"Thought so," Teddy yelled into the night. "But I couldn't be sure in this murk."

A buddy! He needed a friend like that.

Beside him, Vada said in a jiggly voice, "Is—is Homer Hodges going to be here, Loren?"

"Yes," he replied. "He's bringing his girl from Almond Grove. Name's Carol something."

She probably didn't know her. Now her voice seemed even more jiggly, maybe because her teeth were chattering in this freezing cold.

"Loren," she said in her shy style, "when you make out our program card, would you do me a favor?"

"Sure," he answered in a husky voice. He had only this one evening with Vada, so why not be lavish? Let her run things the way she probably would do anyway.

"Will you—would you trade a couple of dances with Homer? I—I'd like to dance with him."

He had to do another take on that one; no girl in Carleton had ever before danced with Hodges willingly. Those who had done it under duress claimed it was like shaking hands with a mechanical corn shucker.

"You—you want to dance with Alice?"

"Oh, yes," she breathed. "I do."

He shrugged. That did it. But who was he to deny? How could a mere youth divine what went on inside of their cute little minds? Well, he couldn't.

They got inside, and Loren located various teachers prowling around, snatching cookies, guzzling punch, and robbing the good. That way, he could decide which direction to go. Away.

He fixed up a fairly good program with the only trouble coming from an unexpected source—Hodges. He had brought this tall, red-haired girl.

Alice had a far-out expression, which on him didn't look too human. "Man, that there's a true woman," he moaned like a foghorn at bay. "She's got to me. I dunno. I'll let go of one dance for a pal. But two? Unh-unh. I wanna keep her for myself, get it?"

Vada had said two, so Loren persisted.

Hodges argued awhile, but he finally gave in. "All right, all right," he said. "Two. I can sacrifice myself and jog around with that skinny little colorless Vada, I guess. So shut up, Loren. Quit nagging. You irritate a guy, see?"

Later, the orchestra started the first number, and teachers jumped back, startled, as the deep tones of the electric guitar actually hit. Loren found Vada, and they danced together in silence, mainly because the music was too loud for talk, and also he was trying to get his feet to understand each other. When they did it, he risked glancing down. Then he gulped.

There was a silky, soft, and wonderful quality in her eyes, and her lips had a knowing, inward expression he hadn't seen before. Why, she was—

"I—" he began.

The dance ended there, so he couldn't finish. But he faced one truth: there was no use in pretending he didn't care whether she was Morgan's girl. He did; he cared a lot, and although she was as distant from him as those stars tonight, he wanted to tell her somehow that he was glad he knew her.

Loren danced with Shirlee, Jacoby's girl, and with Laneva, who had come with Tuthouse. The whole time, he watched those guys with Vada, and it hit him that he'd misjudged them both.

Jacoby was looking down at her, giving with his smooth, suave yak, and it occurred to Loren that there was a sinister cast to Teddy's so-called countenance he'd never noticed before. His mouth flapped like flannel in a breeze. Up close, it was a horrible sight that could enrage a friend if he had to look at it too much.

Also Tuthouse wasn't so fine, either. Lardboy's dancing expression was completely idiotic, and when he saw Vada giggling at the character's presumed wit, Loren ground his teeth. What she could see in Tuthouse was more than he'd ever know in life.

It was time to dance with the girl Hodges had brought, and she was easy to find. A person could spot that female across the whole gym. Well, he had the duty. He plowed over that way, and suddenly Vada appeared.

"Carol," she said in her silvery voice, "this is Loren. You know, I was telling you about him. Loren, Carol Morgan, who is—"

She couldn't finish, because the music began again, now much softer. Mr. Hipper and Miss Terwilliger had gone over to the combo and had a little talk with their leader.

Out on the floor, Carol sort of smiled at him. "So you're a friend of my little cousin Vada, are you?"

He thought that over. Everybody had cousins, and some of them could be friends. "I guess," he told her.

"I'm Bobby Morgan's sister," she said next. "I watched that game last Saturday. Me, oh, my, but Bobby was mad."

"Sorry," Loren told her. No use for football postmortems when a person's life could be at stake. A guy could slip and get trampled in this mob.

"We saw you at the drive-in one night," Carol rambled on. "We honked, but you wouldn't turn around."

Yak, yak, yak. Women did it all the time. He closed earflaps from the inside and attempted to see where Vada was with Hodges. He located the guy, mainly staying in one place and marking time, up and down and sort of sideways. Alice had a strained, white look on his face while he peered around this way and that like a caged gorilla. "Ha-ha," Loren chuckled to himself softly. It served Hodges right for bringing this woman basketball forward to a dance.

. The number ended, and he gave sky-girl back to Alice. Walking away, he saw that Vada was over there talking. Carol was shaking her red hair and looping a motion around her forehead, like cuckoo. So let her; the feeling was maybe mutual.

Later, he danced with Vada again. "You—" she said, picking up their conversation.

"Nothing—" he told her.

Midway through it, they were near the punch bowl, so he stopped and got her a glass of the bubbly stuff, mostly ginger ale and fruit juice. Not bad, but milk would be better. He had about five cupfuls to slake thirst, and he ate a few home economics rocky-road cookies. They were fairly heavy on the rocks.

It was time for his second dance with Carol, but before Alice turned her over to him, the guy sort of snarled into an ear.

"I seen you, Wallace," he sneered, "trying to give my woman all that talk you got. Lay off, you hear? I'm watching you all the time."

Loren was willing to keep quiet, but would this Carol let him? No. Out on the floor, she seemed to have a message for the multitude.

"Loren," she screeched, sort of pronouncing her syllables one at a time like somebody's kindergarten teacher, "I'm—Vada's—cous-in. I'm—Bobby—Morgan's—sis-ter. That—makes—Bobby—Vada's—cous-in—too, doesn't—it?"

"Yes," he replied, trying to evade her grasp. Alice had danced up close in his vertical but horizontal style to give him the killer eyeball.

"Are—you—sure?" Carol asked.

He turned all her cousin yak over in his mind. Carefully. It was logical. If Carol was Vada's cousin and Bobby Morgan's sister, that meant—

"Hey!" he exclaimed as understanding hit him like a wave. "You—you mean that Vada is Bobby Morgan's cousin?"

"Whew!" Carol yelled, breathing hard. "Finally. At last it penetrated. I see why she wanted me to tell you. Yes, Loren, we're all cousins because we're related that way, sort of. Kind of like relatives, and all. Do you get it? My mother is Mrs. Long's sister, the same way your uncle is probably—"

The punch bowl was close again, and he danced Carol over there while the music stopped and Alice Hodges claimed his girl.

"I saw you, Wallace," he hissed. "Don't think I'm for-gettin' this here sneaky style you got."

He wouldn't, either. That way, Alice was a regular elephant.

But Loren didn't even hear him. He was stunned. So she wasn't Morgan's girl, after all! If he could only have known it sooner, he might have had a chance, but now she would probably never forgive him for being such a stupe.

He kept to the program for three more rounds, but finally it was the last dance—with Vada. She was here in his arms, as light as cottonwood down, with the rosebuds he'd given her looking fresher than all the roses until now.

He wished he knew what to say to such a girl. The words were all in him somewhere, locked up and sealed—but they pressed him painfully.

"Vada—" he began, humbly.

Her eyes were dark in the shadow of her lashes, but suddenly she opened them and smiled. And, man, it was dawn.

164

"Hi, Loren," she said. "It's—it's been a perfect evening. And now it's over—"

Not quite. The Football Frolic ended, as it had to before everyone collapsed from electric guitar nerve fatigue.

He took her home, going the long way around as much as he could without her noticing. The moon was higher now, and in its tender, lovely light he could see—he could see his girl.

She was kind of scrooched up in the corner of the seat, as comfortable and graceful as a kitten might be while the lights of this car made a golden island out of one hunk of ground that moved through dark and silent streets.

A yearning possessed Loren Wallace, a sense of living in this great old world and being free. He wished they could drive on and on this way, alone and together for always. But that wasn't possible in Carleton; if a person took a girl home in this town, he got there sooner than he expected.

Here was her house, so he had to open the gate again. When he got back in the car, she had changed positions, but it wasn't until they were into the driveway that he realized how close she was. Maybe only five or six inches from him.

The house was stone dark. He stopped the car in front and cut the engine. For a second, he sat very still, listening to the ticking engine noise as it cooled, and the beating of his own heart.

"Hey!" Loren said. Just ahead of the car, a huge shape rose up from nowhere and went crashing away.

Beside him, he heard a giggle. "It's just Henry," Vada told him softly. "He likes to scare people."

"Henry?"

"That Hereford calf I was telling you about. He enjoys being around the house—especially in the rose garden—and places."

"Likes it around the—" Loren whispered hoarsely. "No. It can't be Wal—"

"Who?"

"N-nobody," he stammered. "I was just talking—uh—to myself."

She laughed. "And do you know," she chattered on, "we got Henry in the strangest way. One morning Father woke up, and there he was at the back door, sort of sitting up and begging. Truly. We advertised for days and days in the papers, but nobody ever claimed him. That's the odd part. He's been here ever since." She smiled and shook her head ruefully. "Now we don't know what to do with him. We just can't sell him, he's so cute, and he's getting so big, and—and sort of fierce-looking that some people don't even like to come here unless Henry's locked up in the permanent pasture. But he's really gentle, and I simply won't let Daddy s-sell him for—" She stopped. Henry's future in that direction was mighty grim.

A chill traveled up Loren's spine and tingled there. "Walter," he said silently. "They call you Henry now."

For a second, he wondered what he should do and why his dad hadn't seen Mr. Long's advertisement. Yet he knew why all along, and that there are times in this life when silence is wisdom's eloquent language.

Aloud, he remarked: "It is funny. I mean that Walt—or Henry, should have come here. Of course, it's only across the riv—"

"Across the what? What do you mean, Loren?" she asked, looking up at him.

"Noth—" he began, turning toward her.

And then it happened—probably the way Walter would have done if he were a human. That calf had a style to him.

"Hi—" he said.

Maybe it was how the moonlight lay across her up-

166

turned face, molding her lips in a special way and hiding her eyes in violet and dreams. Or it could have been that Loren flipped right along with the rest of the people in Carleton. He took a far-out chance.

Anyway, he kissed her and she didn't get mad.

Then he took her to the house.

"'Night," she told him softly, "and thank you, thank you for a wonderful evening."

She touched the rosebuds of her corsage as if they were precious to her, and went inside and closed the door.

But that wasn't the last that was said. When he closed the gate behind him, far off in the field Loren could see a hulk moving around in the night, sticking close to home.

"So long, Walter," he whispered, "see you later."

Walter hadn't gone off into the hills to join the wild cattle of storm and tempest. He'd merely crossed the river to visit a friend and decided to stay awhile.

He gunned the little car and hit the road. He was tired—but happy too, as who wouldn't be who had a girl like Vada Long. A woman who was beautiful, all right, and kind to dumb animals who had somehow taken a walk and lost their way home.